Mollyockett

by

PAT STEWART

Pat Stewart

First published in the United States of America by:

Twin Lights Publishers, Inc.
10 Hale Street
Rockport, Massachusetts 01966
Telephone: (978) 546-7398
http://www.twinlightspub.com

ISBN: 1-885435-43-6

10 9 8 7 6 5 4 3 2 1

Frontispiece: Abenaki Madonna
This elegant carved portrayal of St. Mary as an Abenaki
woman stands at the front of the Abenaki Church in
Odanak, Quebec. Although there is no documented
picture of her, the statue suggests how Mollyockett may
have looked.

Book design by
SYP Design & Production, Inc.
http://www.sypdesign.com

Printed in Canada

ACKNOWLEDGMENTS

Since I am neither a historian nor a fiction writer by training, I have had to rely heavily on "the kindness of strangers" as well as friends and family. First, I owe a huge debt of gratitude to the resources of the Bethel Historical Society and Regional History Center in Bethel, Maine. Cathy Newell's monograph, *Molly Ockett,* provided the historical backbone for this fictional reconstruction. The files of the Society's Reference Library added rich information, especially the correspondence of two Bethel historians, Eva Bean and Helen Leadbeater. Executive Director, Stan Howe, provided encouragement. Randy Bennett, the Society's Curator of Collections, not only hunted up old photos and illustrations, but read the manuscript and provided many helpful comments. Society staff member, Dana Nickerson, also helped find old photos.

Bunny McBride, an expert on Northeastern Indian women and author of *Women of the Dawn,* was kind enough to read the manuscript and offer suggestions from a historical perspective. My youngest daughter, Victoria Stewart, a playwright, added aesthetic counsel. Mary Ellen Gartner used her eagle editorial eye to watch out for errors in punctuation, grammar and usage. Susan Herlihy translated Marie Marguerite's baptismal certificate from eighteenth century French. Maine author, Alice Arlen, read the manuscript and urged me on. Thanks also to Arnold Neptune, Curator of the Abenaki Museum at Old Town, Maine, and William Fowler, Executive Director of the Massachusetts Historical Society, for sharing their expertise and informed speculations in response to my questions, particularly on Abenaki culture and spirituality and the mysterious Colonel Clark. Stephanie Philbrick of the Maine Historical Society located a slide of Mollyockett's purse and made arrangements with the Maine State Museum, which currently possesses the purse, to send me the photo used as the cover of this book.

I also thank my husband, Henry Stewart, for his support and patient interest throughout five years of research and writing. Together we explored Odanak, tracked down documents in Quebec, climbed up Jockey Cap and scoured book stores and museums to find books, Abenaki artifacts and other resources.

For Henry
Amor vincit omnia

ILLUSTRATIONS AND MAPS

O Great Spirit, whose voice I hear in the winds and whose breath gives life to all the world, hear me!

Let me walk in beauty. Allow my eyes to behold the golden dawn and the red and purple sunset. Make my hands respect the things you have made, my ears sharp to hear your voice.

Make me wise so that I may understand things you have taught my people, the lesson you have hidden in every leaf and rock.

I seek strength not to be superior to my brothers but to be able to fight my greatest enemy, myself.

Make me ever ready to come to you with straight eyes, so when life fades like the setting sun, my spirit may come to you without shame.

Adapted from an Abenaki prayer, originally in French

Overview

Mollyockett was the last surviving member of the Pequawket tribe, a branch of the Abenaki Indians, who had inhabited the Northeast for many generations. Some said Mollyockett lived more than a hundred years because she often told stories of events that not even the oldest New Englander could recall. She filled tales of the Lovewell Massacre, the French and Indian War, Rogers' Raid, the feats of the great Chief Paugus and buried treasure with intimate details and compelling emotion. Her vivid descriptions convinced eager listeners gathered around a campfire or hearth that she had witnessed each scene of butchery, bravery and adventure.

Despite this apparent evidence of longevity and her deeply lined visage, Mollyockett moved with grace and strength until the last weeks of her life. She was proud of her erect posture, and purposeful gait. One contemporary described her as "pretty" and "genteel." The lines around her mouth and eyes indicated years of smiling or squinting into the sun, but the flesh of her cheeks, chin and forehead remained smooth. Her dark brown eyes sparkled and, until her final near blindness, she saw clearly, noting details of action and nuances of expression. She lived a long, strenuous, eventful life, but she maintained her erect posture and animation of spirit until the very end.

Year after year, Mollyockett doctored the few remaining members of the New England Abenaki tribes still hunting or settled throughout the Northeast and Canada. She also healed and comforted thousands of white settlers living in small towns or on isolated farmsteads. Using traditional herbal remedies, she treated wounds, disease, and old age. She delivered babies. She saved the life of the infant Hannibal Hamlin, who became Governor of Maine and Abraham Lincoln's Vice President. She was a wife and mother. She healed her own son Piol, nearly dead after a fight, and cured Henry Tufts' debilitating illness. She warned potential victims of the last Indian raid in New England of approaching danger and saved them from slaughter.

Besides practicing her prodigious medical skills, she conducted a lucrative business trading the furs and skins of animals she hunted throughout Northeastern forests. She wove intricate baskets and skillfully molded pottery vessels that looked like fine china. She created beautiful woven textiles combining dyed moose hair yarn and porcupine quills.

Baptized by Roman Catholic missionaries, she observed Church practices and sacraments. For years she returned annually to the St. Francis mission at Odanak, Canada, for confession and absolution. Once she travelled that long distance to seek the release of her first husband's soul from Purgatory. When she lived in white communities like Bethel and Andover, Maine, she attended Protestant services. She described the Methodists as "dreadful clever." In addition, like her forebears, she demonstrated profound respect and appreciation for the natural world.

Even during her later years, Mollyockett continued to travel. She often covered twenty or thirty miles a day on foot, or more by canoe, hunting for game or herbs, traveling from settlement to settlement through the forests and along the rivers of Connecticut, Massachusetts, Vermont, New Hampshire, Maine, and up to the village of Odanak at the St. Francis mission near Quebec. As she aged, she moved at a slower pace, rested more frequently, but continued to traverse the woodland trails, seeking bloodroot here, birch bark there and pursuing game as necessary. Sometimes she traveled alone, other times with a small band of Indian companions. Very often she stayed in or near white settlements and became well known among the inhabitants as a singularly helpful neighbor.

Had she lived more than a century? More likely her vivid tales reflected a gift for storytelling, an integral part of Indian culture. Through stories artfully told, meaningful events and critical lessons passed from one generation to the next. In reality, Mollyockett was probably about eighty years old when she died in 1816. She is buried in Woodlawn Cemetery in Andover, Maine.

Fifty years after her death, historian Nathaniel Tuckerman True read a tribute to her at the dedication of a gravestone purchased by the women of the Congregational church in Andover. She has never been forgotten. To this day anonymous heirs of early Maine settlers place bundles of sweet grass and bouquets of field flowers on the grassy mound that marks her final resting place.

In telling the story of Mollyockett, I have included many documented historical events she witnessed and people she knew. I have also included stories and speculations recorded in less reliable letters and documents, or passed on by word of mouth. These sources are incomplete and often provide conflicting information. Understandably, large parts of her life remain unknown, and perhaps unknowable.

In these cases, I have tried to imagine her experiences, relationships, and motivations. I have done so with deep respect for a remarkable woman who exemplified ingenuity, wisdom, faith, integrity, loyalty and concern for others.

Chapter 1

The odor of fresh cut cedar mingled with the scent of sweet grass baskets and bunches of medicinal herbs hanging from the rafters. A small fire, circled by stones, sent up occasional wisps of smoke that rose like incense through the hole in the roof. On a bed of furs spread over a layer of lady's bedstraw piled in the corner of the small dwelling lay Mollyockett, the last of the Pequawkets.

Less than six months before, the family of Eliza Swan had sent for Mollyockett. Eliza's grandson, Eben, ran the whole way to Mollyockett's camp on the outskirts of Bethel. "Mollyockett, please come right away. Mama needs you," he gasped. "Granny is failing." Mollyockett packed up her medicines at once and followed him to Eliza's bedside. On the way, she recalled delivering three of Eliza's children, including Eben's father. As Mollyockett entered the Swan homestead, she almost choked at the nacreous odor arising from the pallet where Eliza lay. In earlier days, Eliza's ruddy cheeks, warm smile and unflagging stamina impressed her neighbors. "That Eliza," they said. "She can do anything—sew a fine seam, cook fine pies, raise a fine family and plow a fine straight furrow, better than a man." Now illness and pain had transformed her into a pale, hollow-eyed wraith.

Ignoring the foul stench, Mollyockett moved to the old woman's bedside. She placed one hand gently on Eliza's forehead. With the other hand she raised Eliza's drooping eyelid. Then she took Eliza's hand and felt her pulse, smiling fondly at her long-time friend. "Ah, poor Eliza, I am sorry you are ill. Do you have pain?" Eliza moved uncomfortably and her eyelids flickered. She plucked at the bedcovers with one hand, tightly grasping Mollyockett's hand with the other. Her mouth went slack and her lips quivered, but she did not speak. Mollyockett listened for a moment to Eliza's uneven breathing, assessing her distress. She murmured quietly, "Yes, I thought so. I have brought good medicine. I will see what I can do. Rest a moment, if you can, my friend."

She stepped away to the bench where she had set down her satchel and summoned Eliza's son, Jacob, and daughter-in-law, Martha. These worn pioneers already had more troubles than they could bear. They glanced anxiously at Eliza, a valuable and beloved mainstay of the household. She had tended to the children and baked the bread. Her long experience with the hard life of a settler made her practical advice welcome. When Jacob had announced one November morning that he planned to butcher a mature, stout sow, Eliza had replied, "I'd wait till spring. I see a litter of little hams and sausages in that lady's eyes." Sure enough, the next spring the sow had delivered six healthy piglets. All six thrived and grew plump, assuring food for years to come.

Jacob turned hopefully to Mollyockett. "Mama has been so sick, but she doesn't complain. Now she doesn't eat and seems so weak. Can anything be done? Can you heal her?" Mollyockett looked into Jacob's tired eyes and shook her head sadly. "Eliza has the wasting sickness. I can do little except ease her suffering. It will not be long. God will take her soon."

Mollyockett administered an alder bark tonic to relieve Eliza's pain and sat by her side, wiping the old woman's forehead with a damp linen cloth. The children were shooed outside while Jacob and Martha sat anxiously by the bed. Eliza's breathing became more shallow and her hands lay still. Just at nightfall Eliza opened her eyes wide and gazed straight up toward the ceiling. She whispered, "It has all been a dream," and died. Mollyockett closed Eliza's eyes. She silently thanked God for Eliza's easy death and prayed for her soul.

As she arranged Eliza's body, and straightened the covers, she mused, "I am far older than Eliza. My time cannot be far away. What will dying be like for me?" Now, only a few months later, as she lay in a fragrant wigwam on a bed of bear fur, she was beginning to find out. She remembered the very day her life force began to wane.

Soon after Eliza's death, on the day Nipwaset, the moon, disappeared from the night sky, Mollyockett joined her granddaughter, Abbesqua, her friend, Metallak, his wife Oozaluk, and a small band of Indian companions for a few days of hunting at Beaver Brook near Lake Molechunkamunk. Her son, Piol, known as Captain Susup, usually accompanied his mother. This time he had traveled north with another band of Indians, scouting for a new camp. Molly Susup, Abbesqua's mother, no longer traveled with the band. After her first husband left her, she had married a white farmer and settled into domestic life in the Vermont town of Troy.

Early in the morning on the first day of the hunt, an unseasonable May frost melted quickly. Moccasins sank in the mud as the group prepared cornmeal porridge and bark tea. After breakfast the hunters prepared to leave. As Mollyockett gathered her rifle and gear, her legs gave way and she sank awkwardly to the ground. Her companions dropped their weapons and packs. Abbesqua rushed to her side. "Grandmother, what's wrong?" Waves of numbness moved through Mollyockett's body. Surprised by her inability to stand, she paused before answering. Momentary panic swept away her reason. She thought, "What is wrong, what is wrong? Don't know. Something new to me. Something bad." Then, recovering her senses, she said aloud, "Just a passing weakness, I reckon. I'll be all right. But a little medicine would be good. The feverwort tonic I made last week is in the jug at the bottom of my pack. Give me a dose of that. I'll be fine." She smiled reassuringly. "Yes, a little tonic and I'll be fine."

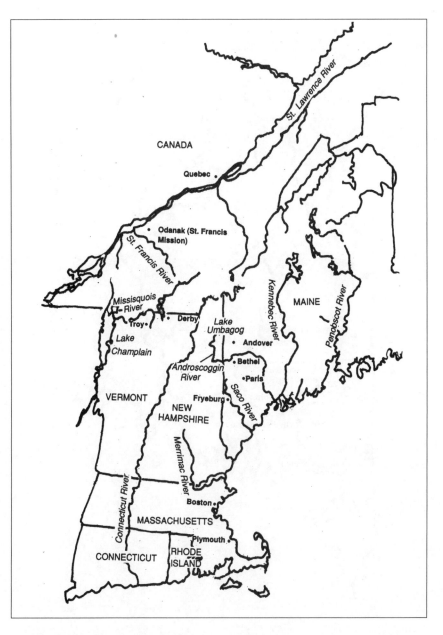

Map of the Territory Mollyockett Traveled on Foot or by Boat or Canoe

During her long life Mollyockett traveled extensively throughout New England. Born in Fryeburg, Maine, she visited and stayed in Indian and white settlements in Connecticut, Vermont, New Hampshire, Massachusetts, Maine and Canada. She died in Andover, Maine in 1816.

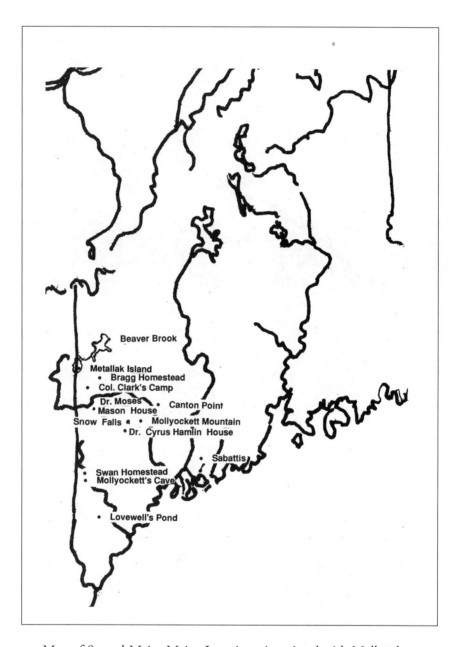

Map of Several Major Maine Locations Associated with Mollyockett

Maine's Route 26, which runs in a northwesterly direction from Gray through Bethel, has been called "The Mollyockett Trail."

Soon after the taste of bitter tonic faded, some strength returned. Mollyockett grunted as she tried to raise herself. She fell back. Abbesqua eased the old woman onto a fur rug. "Grandmother, it's too soon. Rest. We'll wait a bit before we leave." "No, child," Mollyockett objected, "There is no need to waste time or delay the hunt. The season for good hunting is almost over and we need fresh meat. If you leave me with a kettle of tea and a little warm porridge, I will rest and gather strength while you are away."

After some discussion, Mollyockett's companions reluctantly agreed to leave her. Abbesqua rebuilt the fire. Like her grandmother she was tall and comely. She moved with easy grace about the campsite. Because of the morning chill, she still wore leggings under her knee length woolen dress. When the fire was established and embers glowed red, she withdrew hot stones and dropped them into a kettle of water mixed with dried chamomile flowers. She placed the kettle near the flames and warmed some cornmeal porridge in a tin pot. When the water boiled and the porridge was hot, she filled a cup with hot water and dried raspberry leaves to make tea. She poured porridge into a wooden bowl. She set the food near Mollyockett. After watching the old woman take a few swallows of both food and drink, Abbesqua smiled and nodded with satisfaction at Metallak. He returned Abbesqua's smile and consulted Oozaluk quietly. "Do you think she can stay alone?"

Oozaluk was a plain, almost homely woman. What might have seemed harsh features were softened by fine lines from years of smiling. She was heavier than most Indian women, but wore her weight comfortably. Metallak relied on her not only for companionship, but for her thoughtful, straightforward and sensible opinions. Oozaluk looked into Mollyockett's clear eyes and put her hand over the old woman's heart. Its regular beating reassured her. "I think she needs to rest. With any luck, we will not be gone long."

Metallak took Mollyockett's hand in his. "We will return with the heart of a young deer to restore your strength," Metallak assured her. "Good, good." Mollyockett urged. "That is just what I need. Bring back a big one! And shoot me a sweet, juicy partridge while you're at it." Her good humor encouraged them. As they traveled slowly away from the campsite and into the forest, concern for Mollyockett weighed heavier than their rifles and packs.

The band returned to camp near sunset. As the afternoon light faded and shadows lengthened, the temperature dropped. They traveled into a chilly wind that cut through their clothing. The hunt had been successful. Metallak and Oozaluk carried the carcass of a deer slung between two poles. Abbesqua wore several rabbits strung together around her neck. "Grandmother will chide us for not bringing her a partridge," Abbesqua joked as they entered the clearing. She scanned the campsite for movement and worried aloud, "I don't see any sign of her." "Maybe she's gone for a walk," Metallak suggested hopefully.

As they drew closer to the campsite, they saw Mollyockett wrapped in her fur robe, lying by the now dead fire. Abbesqua dropped her rabbits and other burdens and ran to her grandmother's side. The old woman was unconscious and barely breathing. Holding her own breath, Abbesqua felt Mollyockett's face and put her ear to the still beating heart. "She's alive, but she's cold as a stone." The tea in the tin kettle had boiled away and the kettle itself was singed beyond further use. The porridge, except for the first spoonfuls, had not been touched. Abbesqua tried to think calmly. "Let's try dosing her again with some of her herbs, feverfew, I guess, as a start. I'm sure there's some in her pouch. I don't know what else would be good. I wish I paid more attention to grandmother's doctoring. She always knows what to do and now she can't tell me."

Metallak was not much taller than Abbesqua, but powerfully built for a man of sixty-five. His shoulder muscles flexed unconsciously as he wondered whether to move Mollyockett or to leave her where she was. He decided not to disturb her for now. He moved dry branches from a small pile, broke them up and rebuilt the fire.

Meanwhile, Abbesqua searched her grandmother's herb bag and settled on a medicine concocted of feverfew, tansy, sweet flag and balm.

She set a pot of water mixed with herbs and a small amount of rum on the rekindled fire. Meanwhile, Oozaluk quietly began to skin and dress the rabbits. When the brew had steeped, Metallak supported Mollyockett while Abbesqua spooned the medicine into her grandmother's mouth. Sure enough, Mollyockett slowly regained consciousness. She smelled the steeped herbs; then she felt the rum warming her chest as a visit from an old friend warms the heart. A buzzing sound, like flies newly hatched, gradually became the separate voices of Abbesqua, Metallak and the others. "She's awakening!" "Let her lie down!" "No, keep her propped up. It will make her blood flow better." As her mind cleared, Mollyockett smiled with amusement and approval at her granddaughter. "So you did pay attention when I tried to teach you my cures," she murmured. "You'll be a medicine woman yet!"

Although the herbs and a hastily simmered heart of venison broth revived Mollyockett somewhat, she still could not stand. After two days with no improvement, Mollyockett said, "You must return to the summer camp to plant crops and gather food. Though it is not yet summer, we must begin to prepare for winter. I know I am not strong enough to travel with you this time. It's only a day's journey to Andover. You can leave me there and we'll see what God has in store." Metallak and Joseph Neptune, a young Penobscot, who was traveling with the group, constructed a deer hide litter. They spent the night by the brook and broke camp early the next morning.

Her companions carried Mollyockett along the trail running next to Beaver Brook to the place they had left their canoe. They removed the alder branches covering the canoe and settled Mollyockett into the bow. They paddled with effort on the choppy waters of the larger lake to the narrows and then onto the smaller, quieter lake, where they picked up speed. At the outlet they continued down Black Brook as far as they could. They hid the canoe once again and continued on foot into the Andover settlement on the banks of the Ellis River.

Townspeople gathered as the tattered band of Indians carried their sad burden into the village. Thomas Bragg's family, descendants of one of the town's first settlers, immediately agreed to take Mollyockett into their home and care for her. Generally in such cases the town would reimburse their expenses and pay a little extra to boot. At first Sophia Bragg silently resented her husband's offer. Her days were already long and burdensome with the care of three small children, the house and garden. She complained to herself, "I'll do all the work and he'll get all the money." Her heart softened as she looked down on the tired old Indian. She still treasured the whiteware pudding dish Mollyockett had made for her as a wedding gift. "Well," she thought, "I suppose after all the times she's helped us, that's the least we can do. I'll ask my sister if her Sarah can stay with us to help out for a while."

Sophia wore a patched but tidy homespun dress. She retied her apron, straightened her cap and set to work. She immediately moved her children's things from the sleeping quarters into the sitting room so Mollyockett could rest quietly outside the central bustle of the household. Other neighbors offered to help. The town elders met. They agreed that if Mollyockett remained with them, the town would pay for her upkeep. Besides a genuine concern for Mollyockett, the settlers knew that if the entire band of Indians stayed in town, they would expect to be fed, as well. Thomas Bragg met with Metallak, Oozaluk and Abbesqua and assured them that they could depart without worry, knowing that the old woman would be well cared for.

Still reluctant to leave, Abbesqua and Metallak's band set up a temporary camp near the edge of town and visited Mollyockett daily. After a week, Mollyockett realized she was not likely to die immediately, but her strength was not returning. As Metallak and Abbesqua squatted by her side, she urged them to leave her. "You must travel with haste to the summer camp, plant your corn, beans and squashes. You will catch many salmon and dry them to prepare for the time when nothing grows and the fish hide under the ice. I will be cared for well by these good people. Don't worry. I will not

wander away." She chuckled at her little joke. Then added reassuringly, "If God wills, I will be here when you return in the fall after
the harvest."

Abbesqua folded her arms across her chest and shook her head.
"Grandmother, the others can go. I will stay near you." Mollyockett
held her granddaughter's gaze and firmly disagreed. "No, Abbesqua.
You go with Metallak and Oozaluk. That is my wish. And I have one
other request. Over the years many of my white friends have vowed
to take care of me in my old age. I see they intend to keep their
promise. I hope not to seem ungrateful, but if the end is near, I
would like to approach death in the same way I have lived. You
know how I dislike dwelling in a house and sleeping in a bed.
Remember when Colonel Clark took me to Boston to live with his
family? What a mistake!" Again she chuckled softly, "I am no indoor
Indian, that is for sure. I cannot rest well in a bed. I always dream
that I am falling."

Still smiling, Mollyockett looked up at her granddaughter. "Ask if
they will build me a small wigwam and a soft resting place on the
ground. Mother Earth often heals those who lie against her breast.
In such a dwelling I will be content to wait for God to take me, if
that is His plan." Tears welled in Abbesqua's eyes, but she brushed
them away. "Grandmother, I am sure you will not die, but I will do
what you ask." She turned away and murmured to herself, "If they
do not agree, I will do it myself."

At first the Braggs protested, "We can't have that poor, sick, old
woman lying on the ground!" They relented when another neighbor,
Thomas' brother, Ingalls, suggested that two or three men could
quickly build a small, tight, cedar dwelling—a shed constructed in a
wigwam form. They could locate the wigwam right next to the Bragg's
homestead. It would be easy to put up and, when the time came, easy
to take down. They procured fresh cedar planks from the sawmill and
built a small but adequate dwelling as Mollyockett requested.

Oozaluk helped Abbesqua settle her grandmother into the sweet
smelling cedar wigwam. The women prepared a comfortable pallet—

furs laid on a generous pile of fragrant straw. They arranged baskets and other modest belongings within reach. Abbesqua hung bunches of borage, feverfew, chamomile, bergamot and sassafras from the rafters to make Mollyockett feel at home. Then she prepared reluctantly for her departure.

Early the next morning while the cool mist was still rising from the fields, Metallak entered the wigwam. He had dressed with care and brushed his long hair back with bear grease. He squatted next to Mollyockett and took her hand. His face, like hers, was deeply etched by years of strenuous living. Once Metallak had tamed a moose weighing several tons and rode the animal majestically through the forest. He had ventured again and again into the wilderness alone and unafraid. He had survived many life and death struggles with men and beasts. But as he surveyed Mollyockett's limp body, he himself felt weak. He blinked back tears, then spoke softly in the Algonquin language.

"This day I am sad to see my long time friend unable to rise. I fear that we will not travel together ever again. We have built and broken many camps and shared many meals. We have struggled with and against the French, with and against the English, with and against Indians of many tribes, but we have never quarreled with each other. Rarely have we even disagreed."

Mollyockett smiled feebly as he continued. "Always I have relied on your skill as you discovered and used the gifts of nature for the good of those around you. Now it seems your own medicines do not restore you. I would do anything to make you well. Our shamans are all dead or impotent, but if you ask, I will travel north to Odanak to find a French priest to pray for you. Or I could ask the white doctor to attend you. What is your wish?"

Mollyockett placed her hand on Metallak's arm and replied quietly, "Metallak, God has whispered to me. Our ancestors call me to them. I am well beyond healing prayers or medicines but I thank you for your offer. Reverend Strickland has already visited and will see that all is done properly by the Book at the last. Please continue as wise uncle to my children and my grandchildren, especially Abbesqua. Pray for my soul in the new life when my time runs out. You must leave, but I have one more favor to ask which I cannot ask of my white friends." He nodded assent as she continued. "Please, prepare a bark burial basket and braided thongs to secure it so I may be laid to rest in the manner of our ancestors." He kissed her on both cheeks. "My friend, I am pleased to do as you ask. I know just the tree we will use, a tall graceful white birch that stands near the brook. I will begin at once." He rose, eager to carry out a task to honor Mollyockett.

Later in the day Metallak returned. He knelt beside Mollyockett and said, "I have done as you asked. Your final bed is ready—white birch on the outside, the smooth darker side inside as a lining. Oozaluk and I have sewn your burial basket with ash splints. Abbesqua cut thongs from the moose hide we prepared in the winter and plaited wrapping braid. She has added beads to the braid and scratched a design of loons and wild geese into the outer layer of the bark. We have made openings on all sides so your spirit may leave when it chooses. Abbesqua has brushed and smoothed your best deerskin tunic and leggings and given them and your embroidered bonnet to Mrs. Bragg. If you do not recover, you will rest forever in beauty as you have lived."

Abbesqua entered the wigwam as Metallak concluded, "I rejoice to see that the Great Spirit is with you and will stay by your side in the days to come. We depart, but we leave you in good, loving hands. Fare well on your great last adventure, witapi, my valued companion."

As Metallak spoke, Abbesqua stood nearby weeping quietly into the hem of her tunic. When he had finished, and rose from Mollyockett's side, Abbesqua took his place. She again declared she would not leave her grandmother. Mollyockett took Abbesqua's hand. "Remember how willful you were as a girl? I am glad those days of worry are over and you have become a fine and sensible woman and a faithful granddaughter. You have satisfied your duty to me and now must turn your attention to others. My silver bracelets and gold medals are in my pack wrapped in a moose skin pouch. They are for you and your mother. Give one also to Oozaluk, who has been a kind friend to me and a faithful wife to Metallak. These tokens are my treasure. They will bring you good fortune. Take my place among our friends, living our way at peace with nature. Help others wherever you travel and leave each place better than you found it."

Abbesqua still wept. Her braids brushed Mollyockett's breast as Abbesqua bent to kiss her grandmother on each ear. Metallak placed his hands on Abbesqua's shoulders. "Abbesqua, as usual, your grandmother is right. She sees the future clearly, and is ready to follow the path we all must walk alone. Come with us. We need you." Reluctantly persuaded, Abbesqua embraced her grandmother and again kissed her cheeks and hands. Moaning softly she left the wigwam. Still struggling to overcome her grief, she joined Metallak and the others as they packed for the fishing ground at Merrymeeting Bay near the mouth of the Androscoggin River.

After Abbesqua and Metallak had departed, Mollyockett lay peacefully among her fur robes, her mind full of thoughts and memories. "So here I lie in the care of the townsfolk of Andover. This is a fitting place to rest, since I have dwelt in this town many times over the years." Each breath brought a rush of recollections. "When I traveled away from the settlement to trap or trade or to return to my former home in Canada, these people were always in my heart. I came back time and again to be with them during happy days filled with sunshine and warmth and through long nights of howling wind. It is good to be here again to see the summer come and go." Her eyes closed for a moment, then fluttered open.

"I am a lucky woman." she mused. "The Godly people of this town remember my service to them over many years in their times of need. And so their hearts are moved by my helplessness. Thomas Bragg and his family have freely offered me a bed in their own home." She chuckled to herself. "Stubborn woman that I am, I asked for my own way. What must they think? Maybe that I'm a crazy old Indian. But they did as I desired. Now I rest peacefully in this sweet cedar wigwam they have built for me to die in."

She sighed and continued breathing shallowly as she considered her condition. "I am not good for much. My legs will not carry me to the fields and forests to seek herbs or healing remedies. I can no longer hunt for deer or trap rabbits or squirrels. A mouse could run across my fur robe and come to no harm. My dim eyes and twisted fingers keep me from weaving rush baskets or sewing birch satchels decorated with the quills of the porcupine. Even the energy and strength that held me erect for so many years has departed."

She closed her eyes and rested briefly. Then her thoughts continued. "I can do little but lie here, recollect the past and wait. Even now, at the end, God blesses me. I rest comfortably, wrapped in the skin of a bear I killed and dressed years ago while still in my prime. I am sheltered from the wind and rain. Sophia's niece, Sarah, brings me food and tends the fire." She shivered. "Still I am always cold. I am cold now, my feet are icy, but I will not dwell on that." She raised her head slightly to see if her feet were still covered by the fur. Reassured, she dozed off.

The old woman slept for a while and then awakened to resume her thoughts. "I grow weaker each day. Soon my savior, Jesus, will come down and carry my soul to heaven. He will lead me to my ancestors and the saints. I can almost see Him clothed in a blue robe, His sacred heart glowing through the fabric just like the painted statue in the mission church. I wonder why the Methodists and Congregationalists don't have statues? It helps to know what Jesus looks like. I am sure he will hold his scarred hands out to me. I also see the Blessed Mother, Mary, standing behind her Son, shining with holy light like the paintings on the mission wall. Nearby I feel the presence of the mighty Glooscap, creator of the earth, as our legends tell. His picture I have never seen, but I have known all about him since I was a child." Her thoughts wandered back over the years.

"The Catholic Fathers at St. Francis chastened me and urged me to forget Glooscap, but I never saw reason to turn my back on him, though some say he turned his back on us. Long before the black robes came, Glooscap lived in the stories of my people and he still abides in our spirit. I imagine that he will rejoice at the arrival of one who loves and honors his creation."

Her attention shifted to her ancestors. She closed her eyes to envision them more clearly. "Now I see Paugus, my tall, handsome grandfather. He towers before me like a mighty, straight tamarack. He bears his war staff in one hand and holds his other hand across his chest. My father, Saquant, the last chief of our tribe, wears his sagamore robe, brilliant with dyed quills and moose hair embroidery. My tall, lovely mother, who made my father's robe, stands beside him. In her best beaded deerskin tunic with the pine tree patterns and her black pointed cap, she looks like a queen." She grunted with satisfaction. "They show no sign of the butchery that ended their lives. They have been resurrected in beauty and in strength as Jesus promised."

"Behind these beloved ones, the Holy Fathers of St. Francis, Piol Susup, my first husband, my dead babies, and departed Indians from all the tribes I have traveled with stand to greet me. Among the crowd I see the white settlers who have fallen along my path beside the great rivers—the Connecticut, the Kennebec, the Androscoggin, the Penobscot and the St. Francis. All those spirits who have gone on before me are chanting, 'Welcome, Marie Agathe, called Mollyockett. Welcome to a place of clear, running water, tall evergreen trees, plentiful game, abundant berries and herbs and harmony among all creatures.'" Her mental images dimmed and evaporated. She ran her fingers over her furry robe and said aloud, "I like this vision. I pray it will be so."

She considered her present situation. "Each morning, this Sarah child brings me fresh spring water, a basket of cornbread and a pot of warm stew. She is a tidy girl. Her ruffled cap is becoming. She wears a brown homespun dress covered in front with a blue checked apron, just like her aunt. There's a pocket under her apron. I wonder what is in it? Needlework perhaps. I imagine she is twelve years or so. Her breasts are beginning to swell beneath her white linen neck kerchief. She will soon be a woman, but she seems to me very young. I like her quiet way. But I am glad to have other company as well."

Her thoughts shifted to her other visitors. "In the late afternoons, when their work is finished, Sophia Bragg, Sarah Merrill and other women of the town sit with me. They pray for my comfort and the health of my soul. They make me tea and porridge or broth and see that I am clean. We talk of people we know or have known. 'Remember when Captain Segar was carried away to Canada by Tomhegan?' We have shared so many sad and happy memories. Yesterday I reminded Sarah of the time we birthed her tiny baby girl, the first white child born in this town. She told me that little Susan will be married next spring to a young man from Rumford! Imagine that—all grown up so soon. Sometimes when I weary, we just sit quietly together. The women sew or knit. I rest. We are joined just as strongly in the peaceful silence of trust and friendship as in the sweet bond of shared memories.

"Now, with young Sarah it is different. I can tell that she fears me, although I have done nothing I know of to alarm her. If she looks at me at all, it is with quick glances from the side or from under her long, dark lashes. She starts each time I move or speak, like a little phoebe. She hurries through her tasks and leaves as quickly as she can." Mollyockett smiled weakly to herself. "Her mother and aunt have, no doubt, instructed her in her Christian duty to care for the sick and elderly. She is trying to be a good girl."

Mollyockett chuckled softly to herself. "Well, I must look frightful to a child. I have no glass, but I expect my face looks like last year's dried apple doll—brown, and warped by deep wrinkles, eyes all but hidden in the sockets. My braids are scanty and not well brushed and oiled. I know too well what I look like. I have sat many hours caring for those who were as I am now, bony, withered and gasping for breath. And I imagine that I no longer smell like sweet cider as I once did, but more like vinegar. Poor child! No wonder she scurries away."

She resumed her silent musing. "I have always tried to walk through life with dignity. It should be no different as I approach death. While I wait for a happy reunion with my ancestors and departed friends, I will do what I can to create a peaceful setting for my final days. If Sarah feels comfortable with this ugly, worn out old woman she tends, she may become an agreeable companion for my last journey. Children like strange tales. I will tell her stories of my life. I will explain to her how it happened that I, Mollyockett, the last full daughter of my tribe, came to die here under her family's care and protection." Content with her plan, Mollyockett closed her eyes and fell into a deep sleep.

Chapter 2

The next morning Sarah entered the wigwam quietly carrying a basket filled with bread and warm porridge. She set down the basket and glanced quickly at Mollyockett. "Good morning, Ma'am. How are you feeling today?" Mollyockett did her best to smile warmly. "Good morning, child. I'm doing tolerably well this morning, thank you." She struggled to raise herself slightly. "Would you open the door flap so I can see outside?" Sarah moved to the front of the small dwelling and pulled aside the leather curtain that covered the entrance. She tied it back with a strip of leather and caught a loop of the strap around a nail.

"Oh," Mollyockett exclaimed, "It's a golden day, full of sunshine and ripening grass. I wish I could walk along the river for a bit. Maybe soon."

"It is a beautiful day," Sarah replied, "but very quiet. The red-winged blackbirds have stopped their racket in the marshes. The chickadees and finches are silent, too. They must be tending eggs and keeping to their nests."

Pleased with Sarah's interest in the natural world, Mollyockett asked, "Are the winter berries forming yet?"

"No," Sarah responded, "The tiny flowers have dropped their

petals and the berries are quite small, probably because of the cold summer so far. Still there seem to be plenty, so the birds that stay with us will have food for the winter."

"Good, good," said Mollyockett. "I have always liked watching the birds, even the hungry hawks, noisy jays and bold crows. Each one has it's own habits and preferences. I believe God made them for our pleasure. The kingfisher always makes me laugh with his too big crested head, his clumsy flight and noisy splashing, then his proud climb low over the water with a trout flapping in his beak. He always seems surprised that he has succeeded. Also, you know, sometimes the birds help us, not only with beautiful song like the robin trilling at dawn or the dove cooing at evening. When the owl hoots, you can be sure small animals are stirring. When turkey buzzards circle, a dead animal lies below and wolves, coyotes or bobcats may be near. When many birds fly south in large flocks, we know that winter will soon be upon us. When the ducks leave the ponds and lakes, we are warned that they will soon freeze over."

Sarah smiled at Mollyockett's observations. She stirred the fire and added shavings, and then twigs, to the embers. Every night Sarah's aunt looked in on Mollyockett to make sure she was comfortable. Before she left, she banked the fire. Even though it was still early June, this seemed likely to be an unusually cold season. Mollyockett chilled easily, so they kept a fire going day and night. Sarah uncovered the bowl of warm cornmeal porridge she had brought in her basket. "Would you like some blueberries on your porridge, Ma'am?"

Mollyockett struggled to sit up again and Sarah assisted her in shifting to a more upright position, resting against a folded blanket. "Blueberries. That sounds wonderful. I'm surprised there are any at this time of the year."

"Oh, these are berries we dried last year," Sarah replied. "I soaked them in warm water to plump them up a bit."

"Well, aren't you a clever girl. I used tricks like that to add a little sweetness to my children's food," said the old woman as she accepted the bowl and spoon and shakily began feeding herself.

Sarah set an iron kettle on the flame to heat water for tea. "Do you want me to help you with your food?" Sarah asked, hoping the answer would be "no." Mollyockett scared her a little. She had been around old people before, but not an old Indian. She had heard stories of what Indians had done to settlers in the old days—killing and scalping and carrying girls like her away to Canada.

Mollyockett saw the tremor of fear pass across Sarah's face and guessed its cause. She shook her head to decline Sarah's offer and rested her breakfast bowl on her lap. "I wonder, Sarah, if a good girl like you ever disobeyed your parents." She paused, noting Sarah's look of surprise. "You don't have to answer. I was just thinking of myself when I was your age. Most of the time I tried to be good, but I guess I had a stubborn streak." Sarah scooped mint leaves into the simmering pot, waited a minute and strained a cup of tea into a mug. She placed it next to Mollyockett's bed. Then she leaned over and straightened the fur robe covering the failing but still substantial body in her charge.

Mollyockett could see that Sarah was having difficulty imagining that such an old person had ever been a child. "Yes, Sarah, I was a young girl like you many years and years ago. When I was about your age, I had quite an adventure. I know that you need to finish your chores, but when you come back at midday, if you like, I will tell you how I traveled to Plymouth in Massachusetts below the Great Bay of Boston many miles from here, and how I lived for five years with another tribe called the Wampanoags, and why I returned to face my parents' anger and disappointment."

Sarah cocked her head and looked at Mollyockett with heightened interest. "When she was my age she traveled all that way! I've never been more than a few miles from Andover," she thought. "Yes, Ma'am," she said. "I would like to hear about that when I come back, but right now I do have to help Aunt Sophia with the laundry." She gathered up the chamber pot. "Is there anything else I can do before I leave?"

Mollyockett smiled. "No, child. Just set that left-over bread near me. I'll have to eat a bit so I'll be strong enough for a good story when you come back. And you don't need to call me 'Ma'am.' Everyone calls me by my Christian name, Mollyockett."

"What a strange Christian name," Sarah thought. She did not know that Mollyockett had been baptized with the name Marie Agathe, French for Mary Agatha. Since the letter "r" is not part of the Algonquin language, her family called her Mali-Agat. To the English settlers this sounded like "Molly Ockett," so "Mollyockett" she became. Puzzled, but curious, Sarah left with the chamber pot in one hand and the empty basket in the other.

Mollyockett watched her go. She lifted the bowl from her lap, finished her porridge, drank her tea and nibbled on the crusty bread. "Well, old woman, you've promised a story," she thought. "You'd better rest up." A few minutes later she dozed off, smiling.

A little before noon, Sarah returned with soup and bread and a cut up apple for Mollyockett's lunch. After Mollyockett had eaten, Sarah helped the invalid onto the chamber pot and discreetly looked away. She wondered if Mollyockett had forgotten about the story, and if so, how to raise the subject. As Sarah settled Mollyockett back onto her bed and propped her up, Mollyockett said, "Do you have time for that story I promised?"

Sarah brightened. "I promised to weed the kitchen garden this afternoon, but Aunt Sophia doesn't expect me for a little while. I would like to hear the story." She brushed her skirts under her and sat on the ground near Mollyockett's side.

Mollyockett began, "I'm sure you know, Sarah, that sometimes what elders expect does not please their children. In fact, even the most obedient daughter sometimes wants to do exactly the opposite of what her parents want. It was so with me when I was your age. Let me tell you how I defied my mother, the chiefs of my tribe, including my father, and even the governor of Massachusetts, and how I did not get my way.

"This all happened well before the war for independence. The United States didn't exist yet. The French had settled in Canada, but hunted and traded over a wide area, including what is now the Maine territory. At the same time British settlers were moving northward, building towns and villages and hunting in the same territory. And all this while my people, a group of tribes called Abenakis, believed that the land really belonged to no one, but to all. Anyone could live or hunt anywhere within the forests and fields we had always lived in. Our elders believed that both the French and the British were wrong to try to mark off pieces of land saying, 'This is mine. No one else can use it.' My people, the Pequawket tribe of the Abenaki, had lived in the area of Fryeburg on the Saco River for countless years without a thought of who owned what. Of course, then both the village and the river were known as 'Pequawket.' I reckon the white settlers disliked this name because it linked the land to us. We called our larger tribe 'People of the Dawnland': That is what the word Abenaki means, 'People of the Dawnland.' In those days Abenaki people of whatever tribe all shared the gifts of forests and rivers. But that was a long time ago.

"After the white explorers and settlers came to the Dawnland, many of our people died of terrible diseases we had not known before. Many others were killed by white men who wanted our hunting and fishing grounds. As the number of Indians went down, the number of white men grew. They were everywhere. Frenchmen came from the north to hunt in our forests. The French traders often dressed like us in buckskin and learned our ways. Many took Indian wives. They also traded rum for beaver pelts and confused our braves with drink. This was very bad. But at the same time, French priests invited us to join their mission churches and even came to live among us at times. The priests saw us as children of God and were eager to tell us about Him. They worked to persuade us to live as the Bible says. Some fathers of the French church put the words of the Bible into the Abenaki language to aid our understanding.

"While the French were traveling from the north, the English came up from settlements around Boston, and from further west, and claimed our land for farms. They did not like the French traders or

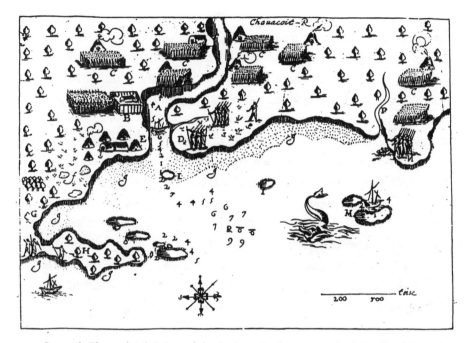

Samuel Champlain's Map of the Indian Settlement at the Mouth of Saco Bay

Champlain drew this view of the Pequawket settlement at the mouth of the Saco River. Mollyockett was born further up the River at Pequawket, now Fryeburg, but probably came to the coast seasonally to fish.

the priests one bit. These English also did not like Indians very much. Unlike the French, many Englishmen treated us like ignorant savages. They wrote many treaties and made many promises but usually did not keep their agreements. At the same time they punished Indians for not living up to promises written in English papers our chiefs could not read and had not understood. Although all white men looked the same to us at first, we soon found the French and English treated us very differently." Mollyockett shifted her position and paused. Sarah watched her eagerly, hoping she would continue.

"I should say in fairness that just as some Frenchmen cheated us and treated us without honor, some Englishmen treated us with respect and became good friends. It was confusing. Good French, bad French, good English, bad English. And then, of course, the French and English hated each other. They constantly fought, mostly over the rights to our land. Indian people soon found that we could not defend our land with either kind of white man if we relied on our tradition of talking together until we arrived at mutual agreement. They did not want to listen to our arguments. If we finally grew angry and tried to overcome their rifles with our arrows we could seldom defeat them. It was a bad time for Indians.

"Still," she continued, "the few remaining people from the many Abenaki tribes, the Penobscots, the Androscoggin, the Wawenock, the Pennacook, the Winnipesaukee, the Cowasuck, the Missisquois, the Sacos, the Sokokis and my own tribe, the Pequawkets, were good hunters, more clever than either the French or the British. Indian hunters soon learned that they could trade furs and animal hides for tools, goods, and most importantly, for guns. With the guns we could hunt better and also better defend our right to live on the land as we always had. In fact, many Indians became good shots and our woodland skills made us valuable as guides and soldiers for both groups of white men as they fought each other." She paused to see whether Sarah was still interested. Sarah leaned forward, eyes wide. Reassured, Mollyockett went on.

"When I was still a child, the British governor in Massachusetts grew angry because the French along the St. Lawrence River to the north had persuaded Indians living in their missions and some members of the six western tribes to raid English settlements. These raids were truly horrifying. Raiders killed and scalped settlers and took captives, especially women and children, back to Canada as proof of success. Many prisoners died on the hard trip north. Those not captured were sometimes killed and scalped because the scalps served as evidence of victory. Prisoners who grew weak along the way were also killed and scalped. The French paid a bounty for both scalps and captives, so more than winning a battle was at stake. Some Indians got rich from these raids. It was a brutal time that no one, white or Indian can boast of."

"It sounds awful! No wonder the governor was upset. What did he do?" Sarah asked.

Mollyockett continued, "Well, actually he did a wise thing. But let me explain the situation a little better. At that time my father was head sachem of the few Pequawkets, about forty in number, who still lived in the Fryeburg area. Others of our tribe had moved north to Canada seeking French protection during earlier wars between the French and English. Besides the Pequawkets, small bands of other Abenaki tribes remained in the Dawnland. The British Governor Shirley called the chiefs and sachems of all the tribes living among the British to Boston. The tribal elders, members of their families and other representatives of the tribes traveled many days to the settlement of Boston at the mouth of the river they call the Charles. I will tell you more about Boston another day.

"The governor and his council treated the sachems with the respect they deserved as the wise leaders of their people. The English government, called the Massachusetts General Court, also honored the sachems with a feast and a parade of soldiers along the Mall and with a show of arms on the Common, a large grassy area not far from the harbor. The parade continued down a main road called Tremont Street to Queen Street and then to the head of King Street where the great Town House stood. Members of the Court, the governor and sachems from the tribes all met in a great hall hung with flags. A portrait of the King of England looked down on the assembly. He was robed in fur with a jeweled amulet on his chest and a feathered hat on his head. My father told us that he found it curious that the English king who lived so far away wore the same sort of clothes as our ceremonial garb: furs and feathers and a totem.

"In an address to the chiefs and sachems, Governor Shirley told of the attacks of the French on his people. He said that once again our common enemies, the Iroquois, the Mohawks and other tribes of the Six Nations in the West, who had done much evil against the Abenaki people in the past, had agreed to fight with the French to destroy the English settlers. He reminded our leaders of their pledges of loyalty to the English King and, in return, the King's promise of protection and rewards to Indians who supported him.

He asked the chiefs and sachems to gather their fighting men and join with the English soldiers in a campaign against the French and the renegade Indians of the Six Nations to drive them forever from the land we shared. Serious matters, dangerous business.

"At the end of his address, the governor presented each tribal elder with a gift of a carved pipe and fancy woven goods in bright red and blue designs. He asked our leaders to think hard about his words and return to him on the following day with a response. A military band played brave music as our elders left the hall, led by a guard of honor. My father said he was impressed with the respect they had been shown. He also said he found the war music, although different from ours, stirring in its own way.

"The chiefs and sachems returned to their encampment set up near the river. That evening they held a council around the central fire. The elders sat together with members of their families and other tribesmen gathered around so all could hear. My father spoke his views as did each of the other leaders of the tribes. My mother told this story many times and I still recall every word. Each leader spoke thoughtfully of the advantages and disadvantages of the governor's proposal. Sawwanamet, chief sachem of the Androscoggin tribe, said, 'The governor and his court have received us with honor and fed us fine food. They have spoken to us as valued friends today, but it has not always been so. As we remember, we have usually been presented with demands, not requests. Also, often in the past we have made agreements and signed treaties, only to have the promises broken. They hold us to our side of the treaty but do not honor their commitments. They have sometimes entered into agreements with Indians who have no authority to speak for others and then tell us that we must obey these empty promises.'

"He nodded to confirm his statements, then continued. 'Remember, my brothers and sisters, how Androscoggin land along the great river was sold for a small amount of grain, worthless trinkets and some rum by tribesmen with no standing who had held no counsel with others. Yet the governor said all Indian people must abide with this false agreement and cede much of our hunting and fishing grounds. As a result of these dealings, I do not trust promises of protection and reward. White men speak like owls but act like crows.'

"Loron, the Tarratine sachem, said he, too, felt uneasy. He reminded the council how, in years past, the great chief, Bomaseen, a Kennebec, had been seized and held as a prisoner in Boston even though no charge could be proved against him. He reminded the other sachems of the white men's treachery. 'Bomaseen, who had always been a friend of the King and promised peace as long as the sun and moon endure, was imprisoned because he was an Indian and for no other reason.'

"Loron sat down and my father stood to speak his turn. My father's voice was always quiet, but deep and got deeper the more serious the matter. This day he spoke like thunder. 'I am no fool. Everything you say is true. We have been wronged in the past, and yet there are other truths we must consider. This is a new governor who asks our help. He is the leader of all the English in the Dawnland and others across the sea who may come in the future. He has addressed us with respect and asked, not demanded, our aid. We must think carefully about his request. Also he says many members of the Six Tribes will fight with the French against the English. These warrior Indians have treated us far worse than the English over the many years we have dealt with each other. We must consider what might happen to our families if the Six Nations prevail. Do you want your wife to become a Seneca slave?'

"Sauquish, a Wawenock sachem, spoke next. 'Saquant speaks wisely. This is a hard question and may well affect every one of our tribesmen in ways we cannot see. Also we must remember that it is not just the Six Nations who will fight with the French. It is also likely that Indian fighting men from St. Francis will accompany French soldiers in this war. These St. Francis Indians are our brothers and cousins. Like many of us they have been taught by the holy fathers and been baptised in the Catholic faith. Can we fight kinsmen to defend white men who do not share our blood?'

"Each chief and sachem spoke his views as the others smoked their new pipes and listened with full attention. The audience also listened intently and nodded agreement or disagreement, but did not interrupt the deliberations. After all had spoken, my father rose again to speak. 'This is a good council. We have discussed many important concerns. I would like to add, that although the English are not my brothers by blood, in our part of the country, some have become brothers through fair dealing, shared work and mutual assistance. I consider many of the settlers along the Androscoggin to be neighbors and friends. Any threat to them is a threat to me and my family. I am willing to do as the governor asks. But I have another worry.'

"He drew on his pipe, expelled the smoke and went on. 'If we go to war, we will no doubt find ourselves away from our own homes much of the time. I fear that my wife and children will be caught in the fighting, and come in harm's way. I suggest that since the governor offers us protection, those who agree to fight ask that he guarantee to protect and shelter our women, children and old people as long as the war lasts.'

"Murmurs of agreement rose from the other sachems. The women in the circle nodded vigorously. The chiefs and sachems agreed to enlist men to fight with the English against the French. In return they would ask not only for payment for their service, but also that the elderly and infirm, as well as women and children, would be taken to a safe place and remain under the protection of the English for the duration of the conflict. The next day the tribal leaders returned to the Town House and presented their response to the governor and his council.

"After all had assembled in the meeting room, the governor invited my father to speak. Regal in his ceremonial robe, my father explained the Indian position in direct, powerful words. Governor Shirley listened attentively. His white curly wig was no less impressive than my father's feathered headdress. His ruffled stock and embroidered coat were no less rich and fine than my father's fringed and beaded tunic and gold amulet. The governor listened, fixing his sharp eyes on my father as he spoke. My father sat down.

"The governor sat still for a moment, then rose and replied, 'My friends, your deliberations are most welcome news. We are honored to have your strength and wisdom on the side of the King. He will be most pleased and will certainly agree to the terms you have proposed. I promise, in his name, that your families will be safe. You can fight bravely without concern for their welfare. A tribe called the Wampanoag lives near the town of Plymouth, a day's journey to the south. In years past, their chief, Massasoit, helped the earliest English settlers to survive. For many years the Wampanoag people have lived in peace with their neighbors.' Some of our elders glanced at each other. They knew the governor was making little of very bad treatment of the Wampanoags during what they called King Philip's War. Still they remained politely silent as Governor Shirley continued.

"'They are good farmers and fishermen and enjoy plentiful harvests. They are more and more our friends and they will help us now. You may send your families to live in the bosom of these people. I will send them gifts and provisions to assure they suffer no loss. I am certain that they will welcome your wives, children and old people as members of their own families.' With this assurance the sachems agreed to provide a body of fighting men to be assembled at Falmouth. This Falmouth, Sarah, was the northern town near their homes, not the other Falmouth located near the Plymouth Colony."

Sarah nodded to show she understood, although she had no sense of the geography Mollyockett knew so well. She had never heard of any Falmouth other than the large town on the Maine coast. She wasn't even sure where that was located.

Mollyockett resumed her story. "Once again the governor presented gifts and led the Indian representatives with pomp and honor through the streets of Boston to the outskirts of the encampment. That night the tribes held a feast with roasted meat, vegetable stews and bread provided by the governor. The governor also sent three casks of rum, which added a warm glow of fellowship to the festivities. The next day our delegates broke camp and returned to their homes.

"At once each chief held a council around a war post and described the governor's request and the sachem's response. Men were invited to join the war parties. Those who did not wish to fight could refuse and remain behind without a loss of respect. Many men, who either supported the English or hated the Six Nations, agreed to join the battle and to send families south for protection. A few decided to remove further into the forest or to relocate their encampments closer to English settlements. It turned out that those who had distrusted the English were right, at least in part. At the same time my father and the other warriors pledged to the King were fighting at the side of English soldiers at the siege of Louisbourg, near Quebec, the colonial government in Massachusetts declared war on all the Indians of the northern territories. So, many of the remaining Indians, fearing loss or bad treatment, decided to join relatives living in the St. Francis community on the St. Lawrence River where most had lived in earlier times. But the women and children and old people of the warriors who did agree to fight were sent, as promised, to the Wampanoags for our safety."

Sarah interrupted, "So that's how you traveled to Plymouth! Did you want to go? What was it like? Were the Wampanoags good to you? Were you lonely, or did you make new friends?"

Mollyockett smiled at this barrage of questions, "I was only a child when my mother started packing for the trip so I didn't think about what I wanted. My sister and most of my friends were going, too, so I helped my mother cheerfully. My father had often been away, hunting or fighting. Although I honored him, I didn't think I would miss him. I had no idea that we were moving for five years and that when I left Plymouth I would be almost a woman." She paused, and continued in a almost inaudible voice. "I also did not know that I would never see my father again."

Sarah sat forward eagerly waiting for more. Mollyockett closed her eyes briefly. "Sarah," she said, "I am a little weary. I will rest now and finish the story another day."

Chapter 3

The door of the Bragg home slammed behind Sarah as she carried lunch toward Mollyockett's cedar wigwam. A week had gone by since Mollyockett promised to tell Sarah of her girlhood adventures. Since then, the old woman had been weak and drowsy most of the time. Every day Sarah hoped the old woman would be well enough to continue. This afternoon the air was chilly and damp, despite the season, so the flap to the wigwam was closed. She pulled it aside while balancing the lunch basket, and said hopefully, "Mollyockett, how are you?"

To Sarah's delight, Mollyockett replied, "I'm just fine, dear. Here set that basket down. I was getting hungry. I think that's a good sign that I will be strong enough to finish the story I started yesterday, if you have time for it." Mollyockett seemed unaware of the time that had elapsed since she began her tale. Sarah did not remind her.

Instead, as Sarah set out Mollyockett's meal, she chattered cheerfully. "I told Aunt Sophia about your adventure. She said you have always been famous as a storyteller and I am lucky that you are willing to talk to me seriously. She also said some of your tales are more like a history lesson and would be good for me. She said I should learn all I can about other people's experiences and about the past.

It helps us understand the present so we can better decide what we should do in the future." She did not relate the rest of Mrs. Bragg's comment. "I'm glad Mollyockett feels like talking," she said. "It may keep the poor thing occupied as she waits for the end. Just keep alert, Sarah, and don't let her tire too much." Sarah promised, but she knew she would have a hard time suggesting Mollyockett should stop her story for any reason.

After Mollyockett finished her bean soup and soda biscuit, Sarah peeled one of the last winter apples and cut it into pieces. She hoped Mollyockett would not notice how wizened it was. As Mollyockett took the first section, she said, "Now where were we? I think we had set out for Plymouth." As she had the time before, Sarah settled on the ground beside Mollyockett and waited.

"Well," Mollyockett began, "as most of the men prepared for war with the French and enemy Indians, a few older people went with the women and children to Plymouth. We traveled down the Androscoggin by canoe to the mouth of the river. Then we walked overland for a short time to Casco Bay. The governor had sent a ship to carry us quickly to the south. I had never seen such a ship. It was bigger than the biggest home here in Andover, and decorated everywhere with polished woodwork and shiny brass fittings. Although I was frightened at the size and speed of the ship at first, I soon could not imagine anything more exciting than life on the sea. The ship was called 'The Golden Swallow.' The name was painted in curved black letters on both sides of the ship toward the back. The breast, head and beak of a sleek, graceful bird with its wings folded back had been carved on the bow. The gilded feathers of the swallow shown in the sun and the bird's great black eyes seemed to search out a safe route. The masts, as tall as hemlocks, supported white sails that puffed out with the slightest breeze. We arrived in Boston in no time, and sailed into a harbor full of ships, many even larger than the 'Golden Swallow' floated beside a long wharf that stuck out, dividing the harbor in two. Warehouses, shops and businesses of all kinds lined the wharf. In the distance I could see many fine homes

View of Boston Harbor in 1830

This is Boston much as Mollyockett saw it on her first visit there as a child on her way to Plymouth.

(From James Henry Stark's *Antique Views of Boston*, originally published in 1882, reissued in 1967)

and churches and a rise they called Beacon Hill. A tower at the top of the hill was lit at night with a bright lamp.

"Boston, too, was at once fearful and thrilling. We had only stopped there to pick up supplies that would go with us to our new home. While the goods were loaded onto the ship, we walked across a short boardwalk with rope railings that formed a path from the ship to the wharf. A young man representing the governor, a Mr. Otis, welcomed us and treated us politely, despite the stares of some of the passers-by. He accompanied us around the biggest town I could ever imagine. A main road called King Street ran through the town. It was lined with small brick houses and shops. Many, many carts and men on horseback rode up and down the cobbled street. You had to keep out of the way or you would be knocked over. Even people on foot seemed in a remarkable hurry as they rushed around in clothing I had never seen—shiny buttons, feathered hats, ruffled skirts made of patterned fabric—so much to look at. My mother urged me along telling me not to stare, but I could tell she was astonished, as well.

"After all this excitement, we returned to the ship. We ate a cold supper and unrolled our bed robes. We quickly fell asleep to the sound of the waves lapping at the sides of the ship. Screeching gulls woke us early the next morning. The seamen had already prepared for departure and we set off for the short trip across the Massachusetts Bay.

"As we pulled out of the shelter of the harbor and into the open sea, a chill wind blew up. The water splashed over the ship's railing as the full sails drove us swiftly along. My mother would not allow me to stand by the rail for fear I would be swept away. As it turned out, I was swept away on this trip, but not in the way she feared.

"We turned to the south and traveled down along the shore, toward Plymouth. We entered another harbor. To the left of the harbor was a tree-covered mound at the end of a spit of land. This came to be called Manomet Hill in honor of an Algonquin tribe who had lived nearby. Another spit of land, with a smaller hill at the end lined the right side of the harbor. We sailed between these protecting arms and pulled into a channel and then into shallower water, near the shore. This time there were no wharves. Beyond the sandy shoreline we could see a village of wigwams and, in the distance, planted fields. These wigwams, unlike ours, had rounded roofs, as if the supporting poles had been bent over and joined. The captain ordered the crew to lower the sails and drop the anchors. We waited as several small boats, launched from the shore, became larger as they approached our ship.

"Seamen threw lines over the side to tie up three of the small boats, each rowed by two strong men. 'Golden Swallow' crewmen lowered food and supplies into the boats and the oarsmen stowed them in the bottom of the boats. Then crewmen attached rope ladders to the railing of the 'Swallow' and dropped them over the side, so the lowest rungs fell into the small boats. They told us to climb over the

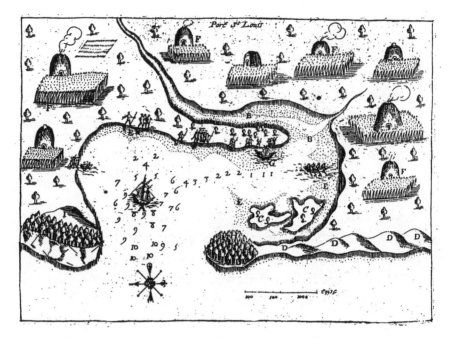

Samuel Champlain's Map of the Indian Village at Plymouth

Following his visit to Plymouth Harbor, then called Port St. Louis, Champlain drew this depth chart of the harbor and depiction of the Indian village on the shore. Much later, Mollyockett stayed in this Wampanoag village while her father fought for the British settlers.

railing and down the ladders to the boats below. The boats seemed very far away us as they bobbed alongside the ship.

"We are a woodland people and climbing down ladders from one ship to another was a new experience which many of our party did not welcome. The old men talked among themselves, muttering that such a descent was undignified. The women, ordinarily brave and uncomplaining, hung back. Finally, one of the seamen swept my three year old cousin, Jean-Louis, into his arms, threw the child over his shoulder, climbed over the rail and down the ladder. As he set the child on a bench in the boat, the little boy began to whimper. His mother, Molly Matilda, was over the side and down the ladder in short order. Following the example of Molly Matilda and Jean-Louis, we all climbed down into the waiting boats. As the boats alongside filled, the oarsmen untied them and pulled off toward shore. The remaining boats took their places and the process repeated till all provisions and passengers were on their way to shore."

Sarah asked, "Weren't you scared?"

Mollyockett smiled. "Well, I suppose so, but by now it seemed that we were moving through life on some course we could not understand. What would be was beyond our control. No point in worrying. Whatever fears we had dried up like a wet footprint on a warm rock.

"A small group of white men and Indians stood on the shore, awaiting our arrival. As each boat entered the surf near the shore, the oarsmen jumped out into the shallow water and pulled the boat up onto the land. We had only to step over the side and onto the sandy beach. Once ashore we hung back uncertainly. Right away, one of the white men came forward and told us, in a friendly way, that he was Thomas Huchinson, a representative of the governor. He led our group to a party of Indian people.

"We knew that these Indians were of the Wampanoag tribe. We did not know much about these people. Their leather clothing resembled ours in style, but was decorated with shells, not quills. Although their language was not the same as ours, we shared enough common words, so that using gestures, we were able to understand each other. The Wampanoag sachems introduced themselves and welcomed us with words and embraces. They were especially respectful to the elders and to those like my mother who were wives of chiefs. More important to me, they were kind to children. They indicated that we should follow them. Some of the men picked up bundles of provisions and moved further ashore. We walked quickly along behind them, eager to see our new home.

"After about fifteen minutes, we found ourselves at the outskirts of a village. The round-roofed wigwams we had seen from the ship surrounded a central clearing. We were comforted to see the usual activity of an Indian village: food cooking over open fires, women grinding corn, children playing with small bows and arrows and husk dolls, old men sitting together and smoking their pipes. Each family group in our party was assigned to a Wampanoag family, who made room for us in their wigwams, for the time being. That night the welcoming Wampanoags shared a feast they had prepared, using some of the provisions the governor had sent, but mainly consisting of roasted lobsters and clams, cornmeal cakes and boiled squash. We ate well, and enjoyed each other's tribal songs and stories after our meal.

"My mother, my little sister, Genevieve, and I, being the family of a chief, moved into the wigwam of one of the sachems, Noamkeg. He stood at the door to welcome us. His wife, Sacawewa, waited inside to show us where we could put our belongings. Their children sat shyly near the door flap. I looked warily at this new family and was surprised to see that although their clothing differed somewhat from ours, we looked very much alike. Noamkeg and Sacawewa, both tall and well formed, could have been my aunt and uncle. Sacawewa smiled as she saw my mother unpack her herbs and medicines. Those who know the art of medicine and healing are always welcome in a household. That night, after prayers for the safety of my father and the other warriors, we slept easily and with little worry for the future.

"We tried to be helpful, but sharing so little space was asking too much of our hosts so, in the weeks that followed we built our own wigwams. They thought our pointed shelters were odd and wondered why we did not bend the tent posts as they did. We began to understand their language and were soon talking easily with each other. As we ate and worked together we learned each other's customs and shared each other's traditional stories. Children from our party soon made friends among the Wampanoag children. My special friend, Alitahasu, was the oldest daughter of Noamkeg and Sacawewa. When I asked about their names, I found out that the Wampanoags did not follow the Catholic practice of taking Christian names. They used Indian names to express qualities of each individual, although some also were called white men's names if they were often among them. Alitahasu's name meant 'She is always thinking.' As I came to know her well, I discovered how wise her parents were to choose this name.

"The longer we lived in Plymouth the happier I became. Everyday life seemed easier along this southern shore. Game and seafood were plentiful. Corn, beans, squash, and pumpkins grew readily over a longer and warmer season. This meant we had more time to play, swim, gather berries, sing and talk. My mother had more time to teach me the uses of plants in preparing medicines. And we learned new remedies from the Wampanoag healers, especially Squana, a very old woman. She showed us how the juice of the beautiful shiny red cranberries harvested from the nearby bogs could help rid the body of harmful fluids. She also showed us how to dry the berries for winter use. Grasses for weaving baskets grew thickly along the shoreline and in the marshes and I used the juice of the cranberries to add a deep red color to designs on my baskets. Best of all, since the Wampanoags now lived peaceably with the colonists, we need not be wary nor distrustful of either Indians or white men.

"Alitahasu and I became close companions. Together with my cousin, Molly-Madeline, and Sally Neptune, a Penobscot girl I had befriended aboard the 'Golden Swallow,' we traveled everywhere together. In summer we swam in the warm water of the bay and wandered along the dunes or dug for clams at the edge of the sea. In winter we gathered in one of the larger wigwams, built for colder weather, and worked together making moccasins or beading leggings. In warmer weather we also worked together hoeing weeds in the growing fields, a job none of us liked. As the years went by and we grew into young women, we talked about who we would marry and the children we would have, and whether they would be boys or girls.

"At about this time I began to take more notice of Alitahasu's brother, Hadomit. He was a year older than Alitahasu and had suddenly grown from a serious boy with a shy smile to a handsome young man, six inches taller than his sister. Although still young, he was one of the best hunters in the village. I liked to watch him practice shooting arrows at a target he had drawn on the stump of an old swamp maple. Soon Hadomit and three of his friends seemed to be with us at every opportunity. The boys helped us carry baskets we suddenly found too heavy to manage. They 'protected' us from any wild animals that might be lurking as we walked through the forest. They brought us pretty shells or bright feathers they had found. Hadomit carved the sign of my tribe, the wild goose, on a clamshell with a hole at the hinge. I wore it on a leather thong around my neck. On several occasions, when Hadomit and I wandered along the dunes away from the others, he pulled me down onto the sand and embraced me in a way that made my heart race. I felt the rush of a feeling that was new to me, but seemed to overcome me whenever Hadomit was near."

Sarah enjoyed Mollyockett's story of young love. Like all girls her age she was beginning to be intensely interested in boys. She didn't really understand why she was suddenly so particular about how her hair was arranged and how tightly her apron was tied. She was curious to learn of the experiences of others, and she certainly couldn't talk to Aunt Sophia. "I guess Indian and white girls are a lot alike when it comes to boys," Sarah thought to herself.

Mollyockett continued, "My friends were enjoying similar experiences with the other young men. When my girl friends and I were alone, the talks about future marriages became more intense. We teased each other and wondered what it would be like to share a wigwam with our chosen companion. My mother began to watch me with concern and made up tasks designed to keep me near her.

"At about this time a messenger arrived to say the English war with the French had ended. The French soldiers and warriors of the Six Tribes were marching back to their homes in the north and west. Soon a treaty of peace would be signed. It was now safe for the Abenaki women, children and old people to return to their homes along the rivers of the Dawnland. My mother and the other elders began to prepare for the trip. She said how happy she would be to see my father and her brothers and to be home once more.

"I was not happy at the prospect of returning to a home I hardly remembered and to a harsher climate. I could not bear the thought of losing my dear friend, Alitahasu, who had become closer than a sister. My own sister, Genevieve, was becoming a pest. I had already decided that Hadomit would be my husband. How could that happen if I lived in the Androscoggin Valley and he lived in Plymouth? It was impossible. The day for our leaving approached. My friends and I talked of nothing else."

"Oh, Mollyockett, how terrible," interrupted Sarah. "I could never be away from my best friend, Grace. And I have a boyfriend, too. James Abbot says someday when he marries, he will build a new farmhouse and clear new fields near his father's. And he says my eyes are pretty. Whatever did you do? How could you bear to leave?"

Mollyockett squinted to bring Sarah's face more clearly into focus. "You do have beautiful eyes, Sarah, James is right about that. I guess you can well imagine how I —how all my friends — felt. It seemed a terrible time, calling for extreme actions. We talked and talked about what to do so we could stay together. We had almost always been obedient daughters. Now we planned rebellion."

Mollyockett paused to recall her youthful defiance. "Remember that I told you the meaning of Alitahasu's name?"

"Yes, I remember," Sarah exclaimed. "It means 'she who is always thinking.'"

"That is the meaning and she earned her name as we tried to figure out what to do," said Mollyockett, a mischievous smile brightening her face. "I declared I was not leaving Plymouth. My mother could go without me. No one could make me go! What a willful girl I was. When I said this to my mother, she was astonished to hear me speak so to her. She firmly explained my duty to my father and to our tribe. She said I must forget this foolishness and pack my things. I cried and carried on so. It shames me to think of the scene I made. My two friends had the same discussion with their mothers, with the same result. We did not know what to do. Then Alitahasu had an idea.

"We guessed that once again a ship would be sent for us. As we pretended to gather berries near the shore, we made secret plans. Alitahasu whispered, 'We will wait till the ship is in the harbor and everyone is packed to go. Then you and Molly-Madeline and Sally will run away and hide. I know a place where no one will find you. You will stay hidden until the ship leaves. My mother and father will be angry and you will probably be punished, but soon the anger will blow away like sand in the wind and we will all be here together. You all can be my sisters and live in my wigwam.'"

Sarah's eyes opened wide with astonishment. "Could you really be that naughty?" she exclaimed. "My parents would whip me if I did anything like that."

Mollyockett shook her head. "It's hard to believe we had the courage, but we followed Alitahasu's plan exactly. When the ship arrived offshore, we ran to our hiding place, covering our tracks as we went. Soon, I heard my mother calling in the distance. I knew she had to leave without me because her place was by my father's side and she had my sister and the rest of the family to think about. I almost ran to her, but I hardened my heart and stayed with my two run-away friends until Alitahasu came to tell us that the ship was out of the harbor and on the open sea. We waited two days before returning to the settlement and the punishment that we knew awaited us."

"Did they beat you?" asked Sarah thinking of the time she had carelessly broken a china cup and had felt her mother's anger.

"No, they didn't," Mollyockett explained. "That is not the Indian way. It was much worse. For a week after our return, we were made to stand alone and silent in front of the wigwams of three important sagamores. Children mocked us, but the elders stared right through us as if we were spirits. Alitahasu and our other friends in the village were forbidden to talk to us. Even after our week of shame, we were treated coolly and without the kindness we had formerly enjoyed. Only Alitahasu's mother, who was fond of me, showed pity. She said I could live with her as her child, if that was my wish.

"I later learned that a messenger had been sent to our tribes to tell them that we had returned to the village and awaited their pleasure. At first our families traveling away from us were worried. When they learned how we had misbehaved, they were ashamed and angry. I heard that my father in the heat of his anger, said, 'Let her live like a snake in that southern swamp!' He soon softened, but the question was how to get us back. Since the agreement for our safe-keeping had been made with Governor Shirley, the chiefs petitioned the governor to see that we were returned in time for the signing of the Peace Treaty at Falmouth in September."

"Was this treaty between the English and the French?" Sarah asked.

"No dear," Mollyockett replied. "I know it's confusing. It was a treaty between the Abenaki and the English."

"But," Sarah interjected, "I thought your father and the other Indian warriors helped the English fight the French!"

"Yes," Mollyockett answered, "That is true, but the English were a curious people. While some Indians were in Canada fighting for the English, the Massachusetts governor declared war on all the Indians of the Northern territory. Fighting continued all the time my father was away. English soldiers hunted down and killed many of our tribesmen, women and children included. By that time we were few and in sorry shape. While we were living peacefully in Plymouth, and my father was fighting with the English in the north, others who had stayed behind lived like hunted animals. Sometimes our warriors, in revenge, would attack a settlement whose fighters had done them harm. It is true that sometimes settlers were killed. More often they were carried north as the Indians fled to the protection of the French. More often it was Indians who were killed or injured. After five years of this, what was left of the chiefs petitioned the governor for peace.

"They met in the late spring with the governor of Massachusetts in the Council Chamber in the Town House in Boston. A great chief, Sawwanamet, stood proudly in his best ceremonial garments.

He said, 'We speak from our hearts the words of sincerity and truth. We have brought with us other credentials than our hearts. These brothers present know that the voice of peace makes Indians everywhere smile and rejoice.' These noble words from the leader of a war weary people seemed to touch the governor's heart. He agreed to peace talks and assigned Thomas Huchinson, John Choate, Israel Williams and James Otis to negotiate on his behalf. Mr. Otis and Mr. Huchinson had treated us well in the past, so the talks began.

"Our sagamores finally agreed to a treaty but said that before the treaty could be signed, all the women, children and old people who had been sent to Plymouth must join them in Falmouth. When our leaders found that not all those granted protection had returned, they reminded the governor that the remaining three girls must also be returned. The governor was annoyed to have to deal with the willfulness of naughty girls, but he had given his word that we would be protected and safely returned. So at the governor's order, a military escort was sent across the bay. An English sloop carried us to Ford Richmond, a trading post on the lower Kennebec River. We were handed over to a group from our tribe who took us back to our village on the bank of the Saco River."

"Thank Goodness!" said Sarah. "You finally returned safely home to your family." She liked stories with happy endings.

"Unfortunately," Mollyockett sighed, "It was not quite so simple.

"I was unaware that as I traveled home a great sadness struck my family. An English farmer who lived far upriver was unaware of the peace agreement. He saw my father come out of the forest with a gun he had been given to fight the French. He mistook Father for a member of one of the hostile tribes. To him all Indians looked alike. Without warning he shot my father through the head. Later, when he learned that my father had fought heroically on behalf of the English, he visited my mother to express his apology and gave her a hunting dog to atone for his mistake. So when I finally arrived home I found my mother grieving and deeply upset. My disobedience was the least of her worries. I, too, grieved. I had loved and respected my father and I believed that somehow I had traded my affection for my friends for my father's life."

Sarah's eyes welled with tears. "Mollyockett, you must have been so sad. I guess you never saw your friends or your father again, but at least you were home with your mother and sister."

The old woman smiled sadly. "Soon I did not even have my home. My mother was overcome by my father's death. She worried about our safety in such an uncertain time. She decided we should leave our village and join a group of Abenakis who were traveling north to seek the protection of the French at the St. Francis mission. She and my father had lived there off and on before they married. Although I was born in Pequawket, now Fryeburg, my parents took me back to be baptised in the church at Odanak by a priest. My father's killer did say he was sorry and tried to make amends by giving us the puppy, but Mother decided that we would no longer be safe in the land where our ancestors had dwelled in peace for generations. So that is how I came to be living at the St. Francis mission at the time of the horror of Rogers' Raid." Her face became immobile with sadness and grief. "You must excuse me, Sarah. That is enough for today. Some other day, I will tell you about one of the most terrifying and sorrowful times of my life."

Chapter 4

After supper while it was still light, James Abbot knocked at the Bragg's door. He had rolled up the sleeves of his homespun shirt to hide the fact that he had outgrown it. The shortness of his gray wool trousers was less easy to disguise. The hems rode above his ankles. He took off his battered round brimmed felt hat as he entered and smiled nervously at Sarah's aunt. His ruddy cheeks were ruddier as a result of a moderately unsuccessful attempt at shaving. His warm brown eyes sparkled with eagerness as he asked if Sarah could come out for a walk. Sophia glanced at her husband as he sat resting from the day's labors. Their young son, Thomas Frye, played with a wooden top near the fireplace and little Sophia sat drowsily in her mother's lap. Baby John had been put to bed and was cooing softly on his way to sleep. As she looked around at her growing family, Sophia wondered if the appearance of this young man reminded her husband of his own first visits to call on her many years ago. He looked up and greeted James, responding in his wife's behalf. "Well, James, I suppose a little walk would be fine. Just make sure you're back by dark." Sophia added, "Sarah is out back feeding the chickens. She'll be finished shortly."

James shifted his weight, wondering what to say. He was relieved to see Sarah enter and set down her feed bucket. Sarah quickly smoothed her hair and removed her apron as she saw James talking with her aunt and uncle. "Good evening, Sarah," James said softly. "Your aunt and uncle say we can walk out a bit if that is agreeable to you."

Sarah smiled inwardly at his good manners and then beamed up at him. "James, I would certainly enjoy a walk this evening. We won't be long, Aunt Sophia, I promise." She said a silent word of thanks that she was not living at home. Her mother and father were very strict and would never agree to let her keep company with a young man.

James followed her as she moved toward the door and removed her shawl from a peg. He awkwardly took the shawl from her and dropped it around her shoulders. As they left, Thomas remarked, "Isn't Sarah a little young for courting? She's only thirteen."

Sophia smiled, "Do you remember how old I was when you began coming around?"

He nodded. "Well, even so, she is young. But we do know his family and he seems a decent lad. Even so, we should keep an eye on them, don't you think?"

"Yes," his wife replied with a wink, "if our family history is any judge, we certainly should." They laughed comfortably together and settled back into their early evening routine.

James and Sarah walked side by side, not touching. Golden beams of sunlight angled through the poplar and birch trees. James commented on the chilly weather that had persisted through the summer. He bemoaned the impact of the weather on the harvest. Sarah listened, but her mind was on the story Mollyockett had told her several days ago. As they reached a favorite path along the river, Sarah said, "James, Saturday Mollyockett told me the most wonderful story. It was happy and unhappy at the same time." She recounted Mollyockett's tale of sanctuary, rebellion and sad restoration to her homeland.

James said, "You don't think about it much, but I reckon some of these old Indians have seen a lot of trouble. But to hear my Pa tell, they caused a lot, too."

"Humph!" replied Sarah, tossing her head, "I don't think I care to hear such talk. I'm sure a white man and an Indian woman might see the same event a whole lot differently."

James was surprised at this expression of feeling from the usually soft spoken Sarah. "Gosh, Sarah, you're probably right, but I hope you won't be so busy with Mollyockett's stories that you'll have no time for me."

Her tone softened immediately. "Oh, James, that won't happen. I do like walking out with you, but her stories are so interesting. I hope she tells me one every day she is well enough."

James flushed. "I guess maybe talking with me about crops and such isn't so entertaining."

Sarah reached out to lightly touch his arm. "You know that isn't what I meant. You're special but she's special, too, in a different way. Don't be upset, because I want to be able to talk to you about what she tells me to help me think about it."

Mollified, he moved her hand gently under his arm and placed it on the inside of his crooked elbow. "One thing rings true. I sure do understand how that Wampanoag boy must have felt about Mollyockett. I bet she was pretty for an Indian."

Sarah agreed emphatically, "I bet she was pretty, period. She has such a fine face. Even with the sickness and all the wrinkles, she is beautiful—high cheekbones, a straight nose, a warm smile—and her eyes! I know she can hardly see, but she looks at me as if she can read my mind and is sort of pleased by what I'm thinking."

"I don't know," James said, "I only saw her when the Indians brought her in and she looked pretty worn out. But since you care so much about her, I hope you'll bring me to meet her some time."

Sarah smiled, "Good idea. I think she'd like that, because I told her about you."

He looked pleased. "Oh, you did, did you? So what did you tell her—how smart and strong I am? Or maybe how uninteresting my conversation is compared to hers?"

She could see he was teasing, so she replied with a knowing smile,

"That's for me to know and for you to find out. You can ask her yourself."

James grinned. "You know Sarah, I'd like to ask Mollyockett about one story I've heard. Or maybe you could."

"And what," Sarah said, "might that be?"

"Well," James began, "lots of folks talk about how Mollyockett buried treasure here and there around the countryside. I've heard that men have searched and dug in likely spots, but no treasure! I'd be really interested to know what Mollyockett has to say. Did she bury treasure? And where the dickens it is? We might get rich!"

Sarah, too, had heard these stories. Surely, if there were treasure Mollyockett would have recovered it by now. Nevertheless, to please James, she said, "Well, I'd guess that's all a lot of hooey. You know how people make up stories. But if I get the chance, I'll bring it up. It won't hurt to ask. Of course, if there is treasure, and we find it, it's really hers and we'd have to return it. She sure doesn't have much money now, that I can see."

They walked arm and arm chatting easily until they got to the place where the path forked, their usual turning place. The young couple lingered long enough for James to brush Sarah's forehead with his lips. "It will be getting dark soon," she reminded him. "We'd better hurry back or my aunt and uncle will be upset."

He looked at her earnestly. "Do you think your folks like me?"

Sarah hesitated. She had overheard her uncle say James was a hard worker and her aunt comment on his good manners. She couldn't tell him that, so she replied, "I imagine they like you well enough. Why do you care?"

He squeezed her hand. "I want everyone you know to like me, including your Indian lady friend." Warmed by their deepening affection for one another, they strolled through the twilight, arriving too quickly back at Sarah's door.

The next afternoon following lunch, Sarah looked expectantly at Mollyockett, who seemed alert and willing to talk. "I don't want to wear you out," she began. "So tell me if you're too tired to go on with your story."

Mollyockett smiled, appreciating Sarah's tactful concern. "No, dear, I feel well today. What do you want to know?"

"Well," said Sarah pensively, "I've been thinking about what you've already told me. It must make you sad to think of your father dying because of a foolish mistake. How could that settler possibly think a dog would make up for the loss of your father?"

Mollyockett was pleased that Sarah empathized with her tragedy. She explained, "Well, Sarah, those were different times. I'm sure he thought he was protecting his own family when he killed my father. He had few belongings, so the gift of a dog was a big thing for him. We grew to love the puppy and believed he showed some of my father's loving nature and fearlessness. We named him 'Little Bear.' My mother said we could take him with us on our journey to St. Francis, and that cheered my little sister and me considerably.

"Within a few days we had broken camp and packed our belongings and supplies of cornmeal and dried meat and fruit into birch bark pails and woven baskets sealed with pitch. These were made cunningly to fit into our canoe and also onto our backs for those times when we would reach carrying places and leave the water for a time. Confusion and grief still clouded my mind so I cannot say for certain what route we followed. I remember leaving Fryeburg. I looked back as we set off in our canoes. The pines that now tower over the plains were small then, just seedlings springing up from our abandoned places for growing corn and squashes. I remember thinking, 'This is the land of my people, of my ancestors, the home of my brave father. Someday, I will return to claim it once more.'

"We stopped at Marankamigoak, a village on the Androscoggin River that we often visited. The English later called the village 'Canton Point.' I guess they had trouble remembering the Indian name. A family from the village decided to join us on our trip north.

"Our seven canoes held a party of more than thirty, including children. Not all were members of the Pequawket tribe. Some were

Sokokis and Penobscots. A few of the party, dressed in ragged buckskins and worn cloth jackets, no one knew much about. Although we realized the trip would be difficult and the climate to the north would be harsh, we departed hoping that we were heading toward a more peaceful life under the protection of the French fathers who had been kind to us in the past.

"After two days journey we reached Sudbury Canada where we would launch our canoes onto the Androscoggin River for a long trip to the west and north. One of the younger children, hearing 'Canada,' thought we had reached our destination and clapped his hands in delight. His mother hushed him and said we still had far to go. What was then Sudbury Canada, a modest settlement of a few families, is now the town of Bethel. I have many friends still living there and many happy memories of that town in later days. I will tell you of my experiences in Bethel another time.

"Because the Androscoggin travels from the mountains to the sea, we were paddling against the current. If we had traveled during the spring floods, or if the wind was against us, we could have made little headway against the current and would have been forced to take a different route. At midsummer the river meanders to the sea so, although paddling took some effort, we moved along at a goodly rate. One person in each canoe stood, using a long pole both to direct the canoe and to drive it forward by shoving against the river bed. At the same time the poler watched for rocks, rapids or shallows and gave warnings or directions to the paddlers.

"We moved at a steady pace through the valley and into the mountains. Once I woke up sobbing. My mother, knowing that I seldom cried or complained, asked, 'Maliagat, what troubles you? Did you have a frightening dream?' Still sobbing I said, 'I wish we did not have to go to Odanak. I miss my friends in Plymouth. I miss Father and now we are leaving the home of my childhood.'

"My mother held me in her arms and dried my tears. She responded wisely, 'Maliagat, in truth, you are returning to the second home of your earliest childhood. Remember that although you

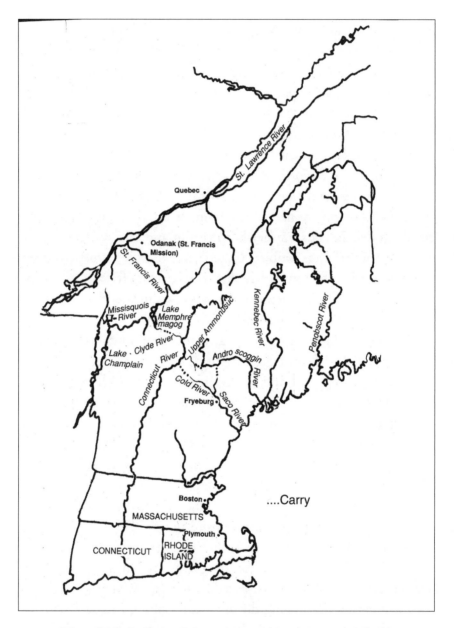

Map of Likely Canoe Routes Between Fryeburg and Odanak

Mollyockett and her family probably took one of these routes from their settlement near Fryeburg to Odanak on the banks of the St. Francis River. Although most of the trip was possible by canoe, several "carries" or portages were required.

(Routes researched by David S. Cook.)

were born below the falls on the Saco River, we did not tarry there for long. Within a month of your first cries we carried you all the way to Odanak to the church to be baptised. That was your first true home and I know you will be welcomed there by family who have never left, and by the holy fathers, who always rejoice at the return of their children. I would not be surprised if a feast is given in our honor.' Then she continued, 'One of the stories in the Bible tells of the son who returns to his home after many years. Do you remember what happened?'

"'Yes,' I replied. 'His father was happy to see his son again. He gave him new clothes to wear and killed a fatted calf to serve at a feast to celebrate his return.' I could see that my mother was pleased that I remembered the Bible story.

"'That's right,' she said, smiling warmly while wiping away my tears. 'You have learned this lesson well. The wanderer was joyfully received back into his family. And so it will be with us.' This cheered me considerably.

"I thought for a moment. 'But mother, the son's brother who stayed at home was jealous that his father honored the son who left home. Will our St. Francis family members be jealous of us?'

"Mother laughed. 'No, my little rabbit. They, too, will welcome us as kinsmen. You know that we gladly receive travelers and share what we have with them. They will be eager to sit with us and hear our stories. You can tell of our trip on the "Golden Swallow" and our stay in Boston.' The corners of her mouth turned up with amusement. 'Please do not tell them of your bad behavior in Plymouth, or I will be laughed at as the mother of a naughty child!' In this way my mother at once assured me I was forgiven, and transformed a moment of sorrow and self pity into days of curiosity and excitement.

"When it was my turn to paddle I pulled as hard as I could and peered eagerly ahead as we rounded each turn in the river. Little Bear lay at my feet in the canoe. I whispered to him, 'You can come to the feast, too, Little Bear, and I will save a choice, juicy bone for

The St. Francis River at Odanak

Mollyockett and other Indians used the St. Francis River as part of a canoe route to get to the St. Francis Mission at Odanak, Quebec. A newer (1828) Indian church stands on the approximate site of the old mission.

(Photo by the author)

you.' His tail thumped against the side of the canoe and he looked back at me to show he understood. My sadness had lifted like the mist rising from a cold pond in the sunlit morning.

"Days later we completed a long carry to the St. Francis River. The river banks were covered with color, yellow centered daisies, orange brushweed, purple vetch and shiny golden buttercups. As we approached our new home, in the village of Odanak, the rounded roof of the church appeared among the trees, topped by a shiny silver cross. I said a silent prayer of thanksgiving to God for our safe arrival and for the gift of a beautiful sunny day. I was about to ask that the feast would be large, the food and games plentiful and new friends everywhere, then decided that was an unworthy and selfish prayer. I asked God's forgiveness. At that moment, a large band of young Indians appeared on the shore, waving and calling welcome. My unspoken prayer seemed to be answered."

Observing that Sarah was still enthralled by her tale, Mollyockett continued. "Before long we were settled among the other Indians living at Odanak. What an odd lot of people! Although the fathers called us all by the name 'Abenaki,' almost all the tribes of the Northeast were represented, including my own Pequawkets, the Missisquois, Cowasucks, Pennacooks, Sokokis, Penobscots and others. The many languages sometimes required patience. Most of us could make ourselves understood in at least two or three Indian languages. Also, most Indians spoke English or French, depending on which group of white men they had dealt with most. Mother spoke our own language and could talk pretty well in any Algonquin tongue. She spoke English because of our home location on the Saco River, but also she had learned French during her earlier stay at Odanak. All of these languages I learned also, even though they are quite different, and it is not easy to speak them all well.

"When we could not make ourselves understood in spoken language, we used signs and gestures. If all else failed, we found others to translate. I have noticed that the English seldom try to understand another language. They either rely on a translator or expect others to learn their tongue. This seems strange to me. The French fathers were eager to learn our languages and wrote down each word and what it meant so they could make the Holy Book understandable to us. For this effort we have always been grateful."

Sarah looked at Mollyockett with a new respect. "I guess I never thought about Indian languages. I just thought there was Indian and English. Some of my schoolmates make fun of the way some Indians talk. Now I see why it is hard for them to speak as we do. I only have to learn one language. Maybe you can teach me some Indian words."

Mollyockett smiled, "Well, you already know the meanings of 'Alitahasu' and 'Abenaki.' And I think I mentioned 'Nipwaset', the moon. That's a start. Now I will teach you how to say 'hello' so we can greet each other. 'Wolokiskot' means, 'It is a good day.' That is how we greet each other."

Sarah frowned. "Wolo, Wolo, what is it?"

Mollyockett repeated, "Wol-o-kis-kot."

"Wolokiskot!" Sarah echoed triumphantly.

"Good, very good," said Mollyockett. "Now, I must rest so I will be strong enough to tell you a tale that still fills me with horror and sadness." A look of alarm passed across Sarah's face. Did she want to hear such a story? As if she read Sarah's thoughts, Mollyockett said, "Yes, it is a bitter tale, but one that must be told." Her eyes fluttered and she fell asleep. Sarah gathered up the dishes and tiptoed out, wondering what Mollyockett could tell her that could be so awful. James's question about buried treasure would just have to wait.

Chapter 5

Several days passed. During this time, Mollyockett had been weak and slept most of the time, but today she felt stronger and her mind was clear. Strange. It was like riding in a canoe in a murky swamp through a bank of mist and then emerging into the sunlight with the water sparkling and the wind blowing against her cheeks. Her lucid state persisted despite the cold rain drizzling outside the wigwam as she awaited Sarah's arrival. She had promised to tell Sarah of one of the worst times of her life. It would have been a fearsome story even if she had made it up, as she sometimes did. It was all the more terrible for being true. She would be careful not to exaggerate or blame unduly, but only to tell what she had seen with her own eyes.

As Sarah entered, cold rain blew in through the open door flap. Her gray wool cape, thrown over her head to protect herself and the meal she brought for Mollyockett, was wet. She set down the food, removed her cape and flipped it up and down outside the door to shake off the rain. She hung it on a peg and prepared to assist Mollyockett with her meal. She was pleased that Mollyockett was sitting up a bit and seemed alert.

"Wolokiskot, Mollyockett," said Sarah. "But really it's not. It's cold and rainy, way too cold for August. You look well today."

Mollyockett smiled, pleased that Sarah had remembered the Indian greeting. Sarah looked at Mollyockett with affection and concern. "You said a few days ago you would tell me of a difficult time in your life. Do you still want to do that? I surely would like to hear the story. I've been wondering about it, but you haven't been well the past few days. Much as I want to hear the story, I don't want you to tire yourself. It's such a dreary day, maybe you'd prefer a cheerier subject or we could just chat a bit."

"Dear child," said Mollyockett. "You are kind and sensitive to the feelings of others. Those are good qualities and will earn you good friends and loving relatives. A promise is a promise. I will tell you of the event that has come to be known by the white men as Rogers' Raid, but truly it should be known as Rogers' Massacre.

"Years passed after we left our home at Fryeburg on the Saco River. My mother, myself and my sister settled into the life of the large Indian community on the banks of the St. Francis River. Several families shared a long lodge. Our lodge housed three other families. We were always with others, although each family had its own fire and sleeping area. Often, especially in the winter, I found the nearness of so many people unpleasant so I sought every opportunity to wander away from the village. When my mother traveled to seek roots and herbs, I accompanied her cheerfully, and when I was old enough, she encouraged me to take such journeys alone. This served me well, for throughout my life I have often traveled alone in peace and happiness, enjoying the beauty of the forests and streams, helping myself respectfully to the gifts of nature.

"It seemed like an uneventful time, but actually people were always coming and going. Some, like us, came to Odanak in order to enjoy the protection we felt the French could provide. Others of various tribes, who had become Christians under the teaching of the Jesuit fathers, maintained settlements elsewhere. No matter how far away they lived, most made the journey back to Odanak at least once a year to make a confession, receive absolution and enjoy the blessings of the Catholic community for a while. Still others came to visit relatives living in Odanak, and to share in companionship at times of feasts and celebrations. These were all peaceful and normal comings and goings.

"But there were also some more sinister and troubling passages into and out of the village. From time to time French soldiers would visit Odanak to recruit warriors. All Indians at this time felt mistreated, because the English settlers had forced them off their land and treated them badly. Around the fire, storytellers recounted memories of raids on our villages, accompanied by the murder of women and children, theft of livestock and the burning of homes. It is not surprising that seeds of revenge sprouted in many hearts."

Sarah's brow wrinkled. "Mollyockett, did you ever feel that way?"

"Well, Sarah, I have often said that as the last surviving member of a tribe who had settled on these lands for generations, I have ownership rights to much of the land now claimed by white men. I believe my people have been deeply wronged, but I have tried not to be a vengeful person. I leave it to God to decide who is right and who is wrong. We will see who gets the best hunting ground in heaven!"

Sarah encouraged Mollyockett to continue. "I'm sorry to interrupt. You were telling about the warriors."

"Yes," she continued, "so as I was saying, some warriors wished only to maintain their honor by avenging wrongs done them and their families. Plain greed drove others. In exchange for supplies and cash bounties, these warriors agreed to join the French in raids on English forts, supply routes and even on towns and individual farms. One of the most famous of these raids on a town had occurred more than fifty years before. Indians from St. Francis traveled south to the Massachusetts town of Deerfield. They entered the settlers' homes, killed some and carried more than a hundred people off. Some captives died on the march north. Despite these losses, more than ninety captives reached the St. Francis settlement.

"Thanks, in part, to the intercessions of the priests, the captives were received with kindness and provided with homes. Some were later sent back to their families in return for ransom or in exchange for French captives held by the English. Abenaki families adopted many captives, especially children, and raised them as members of the household. These adopted captives adjusted speedily to the Indian way of life, learning the language as well as how to prepare food in the Indian manner, how to make tools, tan hides, hunt for game, and for the girls, how to sew and decorate moccasins and other garments.

"In several cases, adopted captives took Indian husbands and wives and started new families. Often when this was so, the captives refused to return to their English families. Walking through the village we saw living reminders of these events—old squaws with braids of frosted gold and children with tan skin, curly, red hair and blue eyes."

"I hope you won't think I'm rude," said Sarah, "but James says that the Indians did terrible things to their captives. Is he right?"

The old woman smiled sadly, "I, too, have heard tales of torture and cruelties done to captives when they arrived at Odanak, but these tales were usually from the mouths of white people who were not there. In fact, I understand that some captives have written stories of their time in Canada. Some have reported a difficult journey full of hardship and loss. But their accounts also tell of good treatment and kind deeds. At the same time it is true that both white and Indian scalps hung from the ridgepoles of many wigwams. These were usually considered trophies of battle justified by the rules of war, and not evidence of wanton cruelty. I imagine that as in all things, the truth lies somewhere between good or evil.

"Anyway, about fifty years ago in September, the cold came early and frost wilted the squash leaves and turned them brown. A good number of warriors left the village to hunt for game to dry for winter provisions. Others, I'm sure, had joined the French to hunt for two-legged game. The women and children and older men and women remained to gather the harvest, dry grain and vegetables and make winter clothes.

"On the day of the new moon, the sky was clear, but dark. We slept soundly in our longhouses. Suddenly, I awoke as if I had heard a voice. I felt a chill, yet nothing seemed amiss. I decided to get up and walk a bit to rid myself of this sense that something was wrong. Little Bear had also awakened and wanted to come with me, but I whispered, 'Stay.' I walked silently beyond the edge of the village and sat on a rock where I sometimes went to be alone and think. Suddenly, I heard gunfire and screams of terror. I was not sure what to do, but I remember thinking, 'If there is trouble, I should see if I can help.' I moved quickly and without a sound to a fringe of alders near the edge of the village. I crouched behind the bushes so that I could see, but not be seen.

"I witnessed a scene of such horror that my heart still tightens when I remember. About a hundred and fifty white men rampaged through the village, entering longhouses, shooting everyone they met. These men were haggard and dressed in ragged clothing. Some wore what was left of their boots tied on with rags. The raiders were filthy and when the wind shifted in my direction, I noticed they smelled of many days without washing. They looked like demons returned from the dead, rather than military men. One hulking man moved among them shouting orders. He, too, was dirty. His clothes barely held together. He was large with broad shoulders. His hair was long and matted. His eyes were cold above a large nose and wolf-like mouth. I later learned that this man was Robert Rogers, ever after called 'the White Devil' by my people.

"As I watched, two of these wretches dragged a woman clutching a baby from her doorway. One held the woman roughly, while the other pulled the baby from her breast. He went into the wigwam and came out with a lighted torch. He had left the baby inside. As the mother screamed in despair, the man lit the bark of the wigwam. It caught fire quickly and was soon swallowed in flames. I could hear the baby crying. The mother struggled with all her strength to save her child. The man holding her thrust the frantic mother from him and raised his gun. He snarled, 'You want to join your papoose? I can oblige.' He shot her in the head. With her last remaining strength she reared up and reached toward the wailing, then collapsed. As thick smoke rose from the wigwam, the crying stopped.

"I pressed my body to the earth under the dense thicket. I did not want to look, but some force made me bear witness to the destruction of my village. They ran from house to house like wild men, knocking old people to the ground with the butts of rifles, killing some and herding others toward the church near the bank of the river.

"I saw a tall man with yellow hair set fire to my wigwam. He turned to look for other targets for harm. His clothes were torn and filthy with swamp muck and other stains, including blood, perhaps his own. His moccasins were tied on with rags and strings. His face, though unlined with age, was gaunt and gray with stubble. Even from a distance I could see his body shift between resolve and fatigue. He kept licking his cracked lips and rubbing his mouth on his sleeve. There was no swagger to him. He held himself erect by sheer will. His trousers hung about his hips, as one who has wasted from illness.

"For a moment I thought I knew him. Could he be John Evans, one of the settlers my family had traded with in the area around Fryeburg? If so, he had come a long way on this mission of destruction. Even as I feared and hated all those who had come to kill us, I felt a moment of pity. Here, I thought, is a man who cannot go on much longer, an almost dead killer. I remembered the vicious despair of foxes caught in a trap without food for days. I flattened myself still further against the ground. I was afraid to stay, afraid to move, afraid of what I might see, and afraid to look away.

"As he staggered away from the burning wigwam, a small child toddled into his path. It was my aunt's boy, Francois. He liked fire but not so much of it. His mother had screamed and fallen. The older children who brought him treats and played with him were nowhere around. He was hungry. He looked silently up at the soldier, eyes wide with dismay, confusion and the unasked question— Will you take care of me?

"The weary soldier gazed down at the child. The White Devil had ordered his men to kill us all, men, women and children. The scare-crow soldier had probably learned to follow orders without question. They were short of ammunition. He raised the musket over his head so he could smash Francois' head with the butt. His eyes swept over the little boy I began to push myself up thinking I could draw his attention away from Francois, but knowing I would probably be killed, too. Then he stopped. Perhaps Francois reminded him of his own child or perhaps he was just too tired, but he slowly lowered the musket and wearily stepped around the child. Francois, unaware of the danger, turned to watch him go and started to follow.

"Just then the White Devil himself entered the clearing. He was as dirty and ragged as the other soldier, but charged with energy, like a lightening bolt. 'Evans!' he roared, 'Why have you not killed that brat?' 'Sir,' the soldier replied, pulling his body erect, 'He's just a baby! I have not the heart to kill him.'

"Rogers shoved Evans aside, shouldered his rifle and shot Francois in the head. Blood gushed over his sweet round face and he fell at Evans' feet. I could hardly keep from crying out. Rogers shook his rifle at Evans and regarded him with anger and disgust. 'You damned fool,' he shouted. 'I said to kill them all. Nits will be lice.'

"Evans' face flushed with shame for a moment, then resumed its worn out pallor. The White Devil glared at his soldier for a moment. Then he said in a lower voice, 'Evans, you've been a good fighter. I know you're tuckered out. We'll forget this, but if it happens again, I'll have no choice but to consider it a dereliction of duty and act accordingly. Now, let's finish this job.' He wheeled around and ran back in the direction he had come.

"Evans looked down at little Francois, bleeding into the dirt. 'I'm sorry, little feller,' he mumbled, 'I don't think this is what General Amherst wanted.' Then he turned and staggered after Rogers. As soon as I was sure they were both gone, I crept out, grabbed Francois and carried him back to my hiding place. I hoped he was not really dead and that I could nurse him back to life as I had once played at healing my corn dolls. I held him to me and prayed, first with the

'Notre Patre' prayer Father Antoine taught us, then a plea to the Great Spirit in my own language. The words did not help Francois come back to life, but they helped me prepare myself for whatever might come.

"With Francois' warm blood staining my tunic, I carried him back into the brush. I could not bury him properly but I knew of a hollow tree that would keep his body safe for a while. I had to tuck his legs and bend his body to ease him sidewise into the cavity. I wrapped his arms around his body as if he were comforting himself with a hug. Now he looked like he was taking a nap in the tree. I whispered, 'Good bye, little brother. I will come for you when I can.'

"I heard the crackling of fire grow louder and turned to see a huge tongue of flame leap into the sky. They had set fire to the church. The cross at the top arch of the roof was engulfed in white smoke. It was too much to bear. Weeping, I ran further into the wood. Soon I found I was not alone. Other villagers had escaped by running into the forest in the midst of the confusion. I asked if anyone had seen my mother or my sister. All shook their heads sadly. Another small group of women who had been captured and forced to watch the burning of the church and murder of a priest made their way into the forest. I learned later that General Amherst, who was in command, had ordered Rogers to take revenge on the Indians, but not to harm women and children. I guess Major Rogers had suddenly remembered his orders.

"Within two hours we saw the raiders leave the village and head down the river. They carried with them silver communion vessels they had stolen from the church and large supplies of corn and dried meat from the village. They also took several white captives who had been living in the village, as well as five Indian children, two boys and three girls. One of the girls was my sister, Genevieve. She died on the trip south. The oldest boy was Sabattis, who later became my husband."

Sarah was near tears. She twisted her apron in her lap. "How awful. How terribly awful! But what about your mother. Surely you were reunited."

Mollyockett's eyes clouded. "I found her near our longhouse. She had been shot as she tried to prevent them from taking my little sister. I learned later from Sabattis that Rogers and his men were unable to return to their boats, because the French had discovered them, so they traveled overland through the spruce swamp. Before they reached Charlestown, the nearest white settlement, many raiders had died of fatigue and starvation. I regret the loss of any life, but I regret these less than most. The White Devil survived to boast of the many Abenaki 'warriors' he had killed. Warriors, indeed. They were all women and children, all women and children. It still pains me to think of it." She closed her eyes then raised herself and seemed to be gathering strength to continue.

Chapter 6

Sarah listened intently to Mollyockett's account of Rogers' Raid on the St. Francis mission. Her face grew pale, her eyes filled with concern. She anguished over the death of little Francois and Mollyockett's mother. The death of her mother! And her father killed like an animal! That made Mollyockett an orphan, alone in what must have seemed a terrifying and brutal world. "Oh, Molly, how awful! How could you bear it? What happened?" Mollyockett reopened her eyes and prepared to tell of events she could never forget.

The old woman rested a moment while Sarah held her breath. Then Mollyockett resumed her story. "For two days after Rogers and his murderous soldiers withdrew across the river, smoke continued to rise from the remains of the church. Our homes burned much more quickly and were reduced to piles of embers within hours. The air was heavy with the odor of burnt flesh, resulting largely from the fiery destruction of the hides that lined our wigwams but also because many of our unfortunate friends and neighbors had died within their own homes.

"Slowly, the surviving villagers left their hiding places and gathered around the ashes of what had been the center of our community life, our church. By some miracle, two of the priests, Father Jean Pierre and Father Tomas had been visiting sick communicants in outlying family settlements. When they saw smoke rising from the area of the village, they returned to find their life's work in ruins and many of their parishioners dead, wounded or carried away.

"With the help of the villagers who were uninjured or less seriously harmed, the priests gathered up the wounded and dying and set up an infirmary. My mind was numb with the horrors I had seen, but my body seemed full of energy. I helped in the sorrowful work of dragging bodies to a place where blankets, mats, and wigwam fragments were laid on the ground. We brought water from the river and bathed and bound wounds as best we could. Father Tomas knelt by each of the dead and dying and said the last rites. Father Jean Pierre remembered that I knew medicines and asked me to see what aids to healing or relief of pain I could find in the remains of the settlement.

"I wept when I found my mother's store of herbs and barks had burned to ashes. Her healing art seemed to have died with her. I felt overcome with sorrow and pain. At first I wanted to hide somewhere and weep. Then I could not be still. I paced back and forth and absently plucked at my tunic. I had to do something! My anguish turned to resolve. I told the priest I would go into the fields and forests to see what I could find that might be of use.

"Father Jean Pierre blessed my plan with a prayer and I prepared to seek helpful herbs. I always carried my gathering knife, as my mother had taught me. I found a charred ash splint carrying basket that would do to hold whatever I might find.

"As I left the village my throat tightened. The last time I had walked here I had traveled with my mother. I easily followed the narrow trail she had shown me. The tiny crimson fruit of the partridge berries lined either edge of the path I walked, but not the very center. The berries had been shaken loose or crushed by my mother and the few others who had gone this way before. Black capped birds flitted overhead, calling 'ko-ko-ki-ki.' But my mind was not on the berries or the birds. A voice in my head kept repeating, 'Can this be true? Is this just a horrible dream?' Eventually, I admitted to myself that the evil I had witnessed was real. Many I loved, including my mother and little Francois, were dead. My sister, Genevieve, had been carried away to who knew where by the most wicked men I had ever seen. I asked God, 'Why is this happening to me? What have I done to deserve such punishment?'

"For a while I stood still, unable to move, my body and soul overcome by sadness and self pity. Then I thought, 'Why am I still alive? Why did not that ragged monster who killed little Francois, kill me?' I prayed to Our Lady who had lost her son to a horrible death. Soon a strange calmness filled my heart. I realized that weeping would not return my family to life. Within the quiet of the forest a calm voice spoke to me, from within or without, I cannot say. 'Maliagat, you have been spared. Be thankful. Use the life you have been given to good purpose. Do not look back at what cannot be changed. Walk forward and do the work before you. Straight is the gate and narrow is the way.'

"From that moment I seemed to gather strength. I knew God was with me and would help me rise above any earthly trouble. I felt my body become more erect, my steps more directed. And yet I had no plan or mindful idea of where I was going. I just felt guided, and moved as if in a trance.

"I was passing along the edge of a stand of birches. The yellow heart shaped leaves quivered in the breeze like tiny flags. As I glanced to my right I saw the dried remains of an abundant growth of bloodroot. The lovely pure white flowers had long since withered. Even the leaves shrivel and almost disappear during the summer, but I knew the fleshy roots remained safely stored beneath the soil. I loosed my gathering knife from its sheath and knelt above the clumps of herbs. Digging carefully, I thanked God for lifting me up in a moment of despair and for showing me this bed of herbs that might ease the suffering of those lying in pain or delirium near the smoking ruins of the church. I gathered a large bunch of roots, being sure to leave plenty, so this patch of healing plants would continue to thrive in future seasons.

"As I arose, I spotted a blackberry thicket just ahead. An early frost had turned the leaves red, but they were still fresh. Bright wintergreen berries lay at my feet and a patch of tansy grew nearby. All three make good medicines. I found myself surrounded by the gifts of nature intended for the good of God's creatures. I set to work, and after several hours of rich harvest, returned to the village to prepare medicines and minister to the sick.

"The dead, I left to the priests. They organized a mass burial and said prayers commending the souls of the victims of the massacre to heaven as martyrs for the faith. The priests laid the cross they had dug from the ashes of the church on the mound of stones covering the grave. This same cross was later retrieved and raised above the spire on a new church.

"By the next day we had gathered what could be used from the remains of our village. Indians from the surrounding area soon learned what had happened and sent help. They brought food and skins and worked with us to build new shelters. Soon more workers and supplies arrived from the mission down the river at Missisquoi. Some of the wounded did not recover, but thanks to the medicines I had been guided to, many survived and grew strong again in body, though many had injured spirits that might never fully mend.

"Before other help arrived, one hunter, who had intended to visit Odanak only overnight, interrupted his search for game to help us rebuild. His name was Pierre Joseph. Like my baptismal name this is difficult to say in our language, so he was called Piol Susup. Because he had led a regiment of Indians who had helped defend Quebec, he bore a military title. He was known by many as Captain Susup. He was older than I, perhaps by more than twenty-five years. I observed his strength, as he cut wigwam poles and bent them together. He was kind to the wounded and offered help in lifting heavy patients so I could tend them.

"I could see the priests thought well of him. They thanked him sincerely for his help, but soon asked him to return to hunting, to resupply the village with meat and hides. This he willingly did. He kept us fed with meat and game birds until the village men, who had been away hunting or fighting, learned of the massacre and returned to assist with rebuilding and restocking the village. When Piol Susup saw we had the means and strength to carry on, he said he would leave to continue his own annual autumn hunt. Many were sorry to see him go. I was sorry, too.

"It was a hard winter as we continued to mourn the loss of our dead and went on with the heavy work of rebuilding our village. I shared a lodging with the remains of the Susup family, who, I learned, were cousins of Piol.

"In early spring Piol returned to Odanak. His hunting and trapping had been successful. He had killed and skinned many deer and caribou. Also he had trapped beaver in the wetlands of Lake Wallagrass. Since he knew that Odanak had been all but destroyed, he carried his hides and pelts to the trading post at Missisquoi. He got good prices, because local warfare had disrupted normal hunting and trapping and the traders were happy to buy his skins. He returned to Odanak with a full purse.

"Naturally, while in Odanak, Piol stayed in the longhouse of his relatives and so we were reacquainted. As we grew to know each other better, Piol told me that he was lonely. His first wife and two children had died years ago of a fever. After a time, he said, he had learned to bear this terrible loss and now he wished to marry again. He asked if I would become his wife."

Sarah wondered what she would do if someone older like Mr. Poor or Mr. Berry asked to marry her. It was impossible to imagine.

Mollyockett continued. "For over a week, I considered his request. I still remembered my feelings for Hadomit, and knew that the affection and respect I felt for Piol was not the same, more like the comfort of waves lapping at the shore than the excitement of a storm on the water. I reasoned that I could not expect the love of a young girl for a handsome boy and the feelings of a young woman, who had lost so much, for an older man to be the same. I knew that Piol behaved responsibly in the village and his opinions were listened to.

He was a successful hunter. He enjoyed rum and spirits on ceremonial occasions, but did not drink to excess. Above all he was kind. Still what I felt for him resembled the love I had felt for my father or my uncle."

Sarah stirred. "What a hard decision," she said. "I hope I'll know what to do when someone asks me to marry." She could not help thinking to herself, "But I hope it's James, not some old man." Then she asked aloud, "Taking a husband is a big step. My mother says it is the most important decision a woman ever makes. What did you say?"

Molly's dim eyes focused on Sarah's earnest face. "Well, child, first I saddened to think I could not discuss this with my mother. Then, after much thought, I went to the temporary chapel set up in one of the long houses. I knelt by the statue of Marie, the Holy Mother of God. This new statue still smelled of sap. It had been carved to replace the one that had burned. This statue was not gilded and painted like the old one, but a devout woman had given up her best embroidered tunic to clothe the Virgin. A fresh evergreen wreath formed a halo. In a long prayer I explained my situation and asked Her what to do. I waited but did not sense a response as I had in the past.

"As I rose from my still unanswered prayer, Father Jean Pierre, who had been tending the altar, addressed me. 'Marie Agathe, my child, you seem troubled. May I hear your confession?'

"I agreed. I began as always, 'Father forgive me for I have sinned.' Because my mind was full of Piol's request, I talked little of my sins and much of my situation. Father Jean Pierre listened attentively and asked thoughtful questions.

"After a while he advised, 'Marie Agathe, you have experienced much pain and sadness in your young life. You are well past the age when young woman usually marry. You should be part of a Christian family, nurtured by the respect and love of a good man. Pierre Joseph is such a man. If you feel affection for him, as you have said you do, accept his offer. I will announce the banns and you can be married within the month. After that, if it is God's desire, you will be blessed with children who will give you joy and comfort.'

"This seemed like the answer I had been praying for. I was reminded that sometimes our prayers are answered through other good people. I thanked Father Jean Pierre for his wisdom, said the rosary and an 'Our Father' as he instructed, and left with a light heart to tell Piol I would be his wife.

"Piol received my answer with pleasure. He embraced me and kissed me on the lips for the first time. Smiling, he asked me to wait a moment. He withdrew into the wigwam and returned in a moment hiding something behind his back. He said, 'Close your eyes.' My heart rose with excitement as I did what he asked. Then I felt a soft cloud fall around my shoulders. 'All right, you can look now,' he said. I was wearing a beautiful cape made entirely of the fur of what trappers called 'le belette a longue queue,' the long tailed weasel. In the winter the brown and gold coat of 'le belette' turns a snowy white, except the tip of the tail which remains black all year. The cape was mostly white, but the black tips of the tail had been sewn around the collar and down the front and around the hem in a beautiful pattern. I had never seen anything like it.

"'It is beautiful!' I exclaimed. 'Where did you get it?'

"'I see you are pleased,' he said, 'and that pleases me. Last winter I came upon a stream where many weasels had their burrows. Because of a warm spell, they ventured out to hunt for mice and voles. They were all wearing their winter coats of white and I got the idea of trapping enough for a cape for you. I was lucky and my traps were full day after day, so you have your cape. I will be proud to see it wrapped around you at our wedding.'

"And so it was. Father Jean Pierre announced our banns for four Sundays and on the first Sunday afternoon in May we were married in the rebuilt church. Piol's family prepared a feast and many neighbors and friends joined in to share the food and wish us well. I wore my cape the whole day. Even though the weather was sunny and bright, the air was still cool. We sang, danced and told stories around the fire.

"Piol's old Uncle Lucien admired my cape. He lit his pipe and said, 'Do you know how the weasel got his white winter coat?' We knew this was an invitation to hear one of the stories handed down by the Abenakis before us. Everyone settled down to listen.

"Uncle Lucien drew on his pipe and threw back his head. As the smoke rose, he began his tale. 'Many years ago when the world was still cold and the earth was covered with ice and snow all year long, Glooscap, creator of the earth, learned that Coyote planned to trick him in some way. Glooscap asked Owl, "Wise Owl, you sit in the tallest pine and consider all you see. Do you know what trick Coyote is planning?" The Owl blinked his eyes and turned his head slowly from shoulder to shoulder, saying, "No-oo, No-oo, No-oo." So Glooscap turned his back on the Owl.

"'Glooscap summoned Hawk, who soared down from the mountain and perched atop a large oak tree. "Stalwart Hawk, you soar high above the earth and view all life on earth with your sharp eyes. Do you know what trick Coyote is planning?" The Hawk stared intently at Glooscap and said, "Naah, Naah, Naah." So Glooscap turned his back on the Hawk.

"'Glooscap called Snake out from his hole under the great rock. "Wily Snake, you hide where other animals cannot see. You observe their secrets and you overhear their intentions. Do you know what trick Coyote is planning?" Snake coiled and uncoiled his scaly body and flicked his tongue in and out. "Yesss, Yesss, Yesss. I know, but I do not tell." Glooscap stamped his foot and the Snake slithered away. By this time Glooscap was losing patience. He thought, I will try once more. If the next animal does not tell me what Coyote plans, I will retaliate against all the animals of the field and forest.

"'Glooscap looked around and spotted Weasel zigzagging across the field, arching his back and leaping playfully over fallen logs. "Cunning Weasel, stop a moment and advise me." Weasel halted at once and approached Glooscap with respect, observing his glorious presence with bright, shining eyes. "How may I help the Mighty Glooscap?" asked the Weasel. Glooscap said, "You travel hither and yon, above and under the earth. You swim in the lakes and streams. Do you know what trick Coyote is planning?" "Well, well, well," the Weasel purred. "I am sorry to say I do not know the answer to your question, but I can find out!" "Good, Weasel," said Glooscap. "Please do so and you shall be rewarded."

"Again Uncle Lucien puffed on his pipe while everyone waited to find out what Weasel would do. Wreathed in smoke, old Lucien continued his tale.

"'Weasel bounded back across the field until he arrived at the rocky place he knew was Coyote's lair. Nearby he saw the burrow of a chipmunk and he squeezed his long body into the tunnel, reversed direction and settled down to await the arrival of Coyote. Before long, Coyote approached, talking to himself, as usual. "Poor me. Poor me. Glooscap has not favored me. I do not have the brains or bushy tail of the fox or the handsome coat and great strength of the wolf. I look like a mangy dog. I have a hard time bringing down my prey without help. But I will get even with him. I will lure Glooscap to the great cave with the promise of many gifts and then when he is inside, I will roll a boulder across the opening. I will not agree to release him until he grants me many wishes. Soon all the animals will admire and respect Coyote!" He licked his matted fur and soon fell asleep.

"'When Weasel heard Coyote snoring, he slipped out of the chipmunk's home and hopped off to tell Glooscap what he had learned. Glooscap was very pleased to have this information. On the next day, Coyote offered Glooscap gifts from the cave. Glooscap readily agreed to follow Coyote. When they arrived at the mouth of the cave, Coyote said, "The gifts are just inside, Mighty Glooscap. I hope you will be pleased." Glooscap thanked Coyote politely. Then he said, "Coyote, my friend, I don't see well in the dark. Go in, look around, and then come back and tell me exactly where the gifts are— to the right?—to the left?—and exactly how far into the cave? That's a good fellow." Flattered and certain he almost had Glooscap where he wanted him, Coyote stepped into the cave.'

"Uncle Lucien looked around the circle and saw all faces turned to him. He paused then made a shoving gesture as he continued. 'At once Glooscap rolled the boulder across the opening, trapping Coyote inside.

"'Coyote howled and complained. "Oooh, Ooh, Ooh! Pooor meee. Poor meee! Oooh-ooo!" Coyote begged to be set free. When Coyote promised never to try to trick Glooscap again, he rolled away the stone. But first Glooscap pronounced a punishment. "Coyote, you have always barked like your cousin, Dog. From now on you will wander the forest moaning and crying, regretting forever the time you tried to trick me." Coyote ran off howling with grief and self pity, his mangy tail between his legs.

"'Glooscap was extremely pleased with Weasel. For days and days, Glooscap pondered how to reward Weasel for his cleverness and loyalty. "He is already smart, swift, a good hunter, cheerful and he has a handsome, dark, glossy coat. What more can I give him?"

"'As the bitterest part of winter approached and the snow covered the earth with a thick white robe, Glooscap saw that just as Weasel hunted smaller animals—mice, voles and squirrels—the larger animals hunted him. Glooscap saw the Owl planning to attack Weasel with his sharp beak. He saw Hawk swoop down, just missing Weasel as he slipped into a burrow. He saw Snake uncoil and spring at Weasel's belly, missing him by inches. And he saw Coyote relentlessly tracking the brown and gold Weasel as he floundered though the deep snow. Suddenly, Glooscap had an idea.

"'He summoned Weasel. "Weasel, you must think me ungrateful for your excellent service. But I have not forgotten your help. I have been trying to come up with a worthy gift. At last I have an idea. From now on, when winter comes and the ground is covered with snow, you will turn snowy white. The Owl and the Hawk, the Snake and the Coyote will look and look, but they will not see you. Further, since you like to burrow into the earth but cannot when the ground is frozen, I will show you how to burrow under the snow. Since you are curious and playful, I will show you how to slide along on the crust of the snow. In the winter, you will be not only swift, but invisible to your enemies. Because, I may need your help on another day, I will leave the tip of your tail black, so I can always find you."

"'And that,' concluded Uncle Lucien, 'is why the weasel is white in winter with a small black tip at the end of his tail.' It seemed the story was over till he added, 'Oh! I forgot to say that Glooscap gave Weasel one more honor. He declared to Weasel, "Men will always seek the fur of animals to cover their bodies, but because I have favored you, your coat will only be worn by kings."'

"Uncle Lucien turned to face me and Piol and said, 'This is why it is right that Mollyockett, who is the daughter of a great chief and a princess of the Abenaki people, is allowed to wear the white weasel cape on her wedding day and throughout her life.'

"Uncle Lucien raised his rum cup, which he had set by his knee. He said to me and Piol and all the others gathered around our fire, 'May God bless the wearer and giver of this royal garment provided by Glooscap and his honored friend, the Weasel. May the Great Spirit guide the steps of Molly and Piol as they walk through life together. May we here who have suffered much rejoice in the creation of a new family among us!' A clamor of assent and warm wishes rose from the wedding guests. Even the children clapped their chubby hands.

"We ate and drank more and told other stories. Soon Piol and I withdrew to a new wigwam he had built in the style of my people. I learned the way of a man with a woman. Before the next spring I was the mother of my first child. It seemed that my life was on a new and beautiful path."

Sarah sat transfixed, her eyes moist, her cheeks glowing. "Oh, Mollyockett, that is a sad story with a happy ending."

Mollyockett nodded slowly, "Yes, It was happy, but it was not an ending, it was just another beginning."

Chapter 7

Several mornings later the sun shone with deceptive warmth, melting the film of frost that coated the ground and glistened on the leaves of the creeping blackberry, clover and other small plants. Frost had damaged crops at least once every month all through the already short growing season. Hail had pelted the fields, punching holes in leaves on squash and pumpkin vines and knocking down corn stalks. Alert farmers had covered tender crops as best they could, but everyone, including the Abbott and Bragg families, worried about this unusual phenomenon. Sarah's aunt and uncle feared God was warning them, or worse, punishing them. On Sunday the minister had preached from the Book of Revelations, "For the great day of His wrath is come; and who shall be able to stand?" He reminded them that St. John had predicted hail as one of the signs of the approaching Day of Judgment. He urged his flock to repent and be saved before it was too late.

The Braggs tried to recall things they might have done or left undone. Since the chill affected everyone, they decided that God was not pointing to them in particular. Nonetheless, they were comforted to have the opportunity to care for Mollyockett, remembering that Jesus urged his people to feed the poor and care for the sick and widowed, saying, "If you do it for the least of these, you do it unto me." One less charitable townsperson muttered, "That old Indian witch is bringing us bad luck." Others silenced him, recalling that the frosts had occurred in all the surrounding area, not just Andover.

Dozing in her cedar wigwam, Mollyockett was unaware of the speculation, although she continuously felt the chill and wondered if she would ever be warm again. She heard Sarah's footsteps approaching and prepared to greet her. Sarah pulled aside the door flap with one hand, balancing Mollyockett's breakfast with the other. "Wolokiskot, Ma'am, You look wide awake this morning! Are you ready for your meal?"

Mollyockett smiled warmly. How lucky she was to have such a cheerful attendant. "Good morning, Sarah. How is it with you today?"

"I'm pretty well, thanks, but a little tired from helping to cover the greens and squashes last night when it got so cold. We did without blankets to save the plants. The pumpkins and root crops will be all right, I reckon, but some of the lettuces and many of the tender herbs look wilted and may be damaged. Uncle Thomas went with Uncle Ingalls to check the orchard this morning. Uncle Thomas says the apples and pears look fine, but we may have to harvest everything earlier than usual or we'll be hungry this winter."

Mollyockett sighed. "I wish I could help. I love to see a field of plump squash and pumpkins ripening to gold and orange and ready for harvest. I was a pretty fair planter and gatherer when I was younger."

"Well, that's interesting," Sarah said. "I thought you moved around a lot. How did you farm?"

Mollyockett pulled her fur robe up to her chin, leaving her thin arms on top of the cover. She considered Sarah's question. "From long before my time, my people lived like the birds, moving according to the season. In the spring we traveled to fishing grounds, generally at the mouth or along the banks of a great river, or near a great fall of water. We fished and also hunted. Then we returned to our villages near large tracts of land we had cleared in the rich river valleys. There we planted corn, beans and squashes.

"In early fall we harvested and prepared our crops for storage. We dried beans and corn. Women ground most of the corn into meal. Other ears we braided together by the husks and hung in each wigwam as a ready food supply. Squash and pumpkins, too, we cut into strips and dried.

"As a young girl, and even after I became a woman, I loved picking berries. We ate strawberries, blueberries, elderberries, blackberries, raspberries. We loved them fresh and juicy, but we also dried many for later use. Women mixed cornmeal with the dried berries. Sometimes we ground dried berries into a sweet powder or sometimes just sprinkled them whole into a maize batter for making delicious corn cakes. When all crops were in, we buried some in underground caches and packed the rest into baskets."

This talk of burying goods nudged Sarah's attention in a different direction. She shifted her position. Mollyockett sensed an unasked question. "Sarah, I'm feeling that you have something on your mind. Is there something you're wondering about?"

"Well," said the girl hesitantly, "Actually, I do have a question. James mentioned some talk about buried treasure. Folks say you buried silver and gold and other valuable things. But no matter how hard people have searched, no one except Mr. Merrill has found anything in all these years."

The corners of Mollyockett's eyes crinkled in amusement. "And what did he find?" she asked.

Sarah recalled the stories she had heard. "Well, they say you told someone that you had sunk an ax into a big old pine tree and then hung a teapot from the handle as a marker over a place you had buried treasure. Mr. Merrill searched for years and never found the tree or the marker. Then one day he noticed a long narrow mound covered with moss and fungi. He figured it was a fallen tree that had become overgrown. He hoped it might be the tree he had been searching for. He dug around it, and sure enough, he found a rusty kettle and an ax head. He dug and dug some more, but found nothing else around that tree but roots. He was pretty mad."

Mollyockett chuckled. "Well, fancy that! He found my kettle and ax!"

"Yes," said Sarah, "but no treasure. Did you hide it there, or maybe someplace nearby?" She tried not to sound too eager.

Mollyockett continued to smile in amusement. "Folks tend to think what they want to believe. I did use that teakettle as a marker, but it was to remind me of a nearby spring where I had gathered delicious watercress. I s'pose that was a treasure of sorts. You are not the first to ask about my 'buried treasure.' Truth is, I did bury things from time to time. We all did. When we moved from one place to another, we often left food or supplies for safekeeping until we returned. When white people assumed our old wigwam poles, spare hides and baskets of grain were treasure, I nodded and gave them a wily look. It was my little joke. I enjoyed the thought of greedy people digging and digging to find the 'treasure' of a poor Indian. White men had taken so much from us already, still they wanted more! Let them dig!"

Sarah laughed. "I see what you mean. I think I'll just keep your joke to myself and let them go on looking." "Good idea, Sarah. I like that. We have a shared secret, like many good friends." Sarah looked fondly at the old woman. "But," she added, "I interrupted. You were telling me about your harvest time."

"That's right," Mollyockett continued. "As winter approached we took down our wigwams and carried everything to winter camps where moose and deer and caribou were plentiful. So we both hunted and grew crops. As a young girl I learned quite a lot about farming. I used all I knew during my years at Odanak."

"Oh, yes." recalled Sarah. "That's where you lived when you were first married. Will you tell me about your life then?"

Mollyockett paused a moment to reflect. "That was so long ago, but I remember it well. Piol Susup and I lived in the family long-house together. He was not a sachem like my father and grandfather, so our space was cramped. I confess sometimes I wished for more, but it is not our way to complain. He was a good man and I grew to love and respect him. In those days it was our custom for a woman to leave her wigwam once a month, when the moon called her, to a special women's house, which no man could enter. After my marriage, I only visited the women's house once.

"When my husband and others noticed that I did not go to the women's house for a time, they smiled knowingly. Piol's Aunt Agnes sat by my fire and instructed me how to care for myself and the baby that was on the way. Everyone gave me choice food and comfortable seating, but still my work was needed so I continued to go to the fields each day. Odanak is so far north that the growing season is short. We had to make the best of it. As soon as the frost left the ground we tilled our fields with pointed sticks and other metal tools the French missionaries gave us. We were lucky to have rich soil along the St. Francis. Still, even fertile land had to be worked to pro-duce bountiful crops. Most seeds were planted in hills because it was easier to till and fertilize smaller areas. Also the crops we grew, espe-cially the beans and squashes, were spreading or climbing plants that lent themselves to such planting.

"We used the heads and tails of the fish we caught to fertilize the vegetables and piled fallen leaves around the plants to prevent weeds. Still, sometimes it seemed that the weeds were determined to outgrow our crops and we worked everyday to pull them out by the roots."

"Well," Sarah interjected, "That sure hasn't changed. I'd be happy not to see another weed, ever! But what about seeds? Our farmers save some seeds from the last year's crop but they also buy some. Where did you get the seeds you planted?"

"We had little money to buy seeds, so at first we depended on other Indian neighbors to share their store. Also each year at harvest time, each family gave a gift of thanksgiving to the priests. The priests kept a supply of food and seeds which they distributed to newcomers and others in need. In earlier years the sachems of each tribe had done much the same thing to assure that no one went hungry while others had plenty. The priests also distributed special kinds of peas and beans sent on the boats from France, but mostly we planted the same seeds we had always grown.

"You may not know that it is the Indians who supplied the early white settlers with the seeds for their first crops. Plants like squashes, pumpkins, corn and tobacco they did not have across the sea where they came from. The settlers were pleased to discover these new crops that grew so abundantly in New England."

Sarah nodded with approval. "That was generous and kind, Mollyockett. I hope the settlers appreciated it."

Mollyockett replied sadly, "The gift of seeds bore unexpected fruit. The white men brought strange ways but they also brought new sicknesses and as our seeds were growing in their gardens, our people began to die by the hundreds. Many whole tribes, like my own, shrank to a few. Some disappeared entirely. Soon our fields along the rich river banks were empty and the white men moved onto land that my people had cleared, planting our fields with seeds that we had given them."

Sarah frowned. "That doesn't seem fair."

Mollyockett shook her head slowly. "No it is not fair, but that is what happened."

Mollyockett realized that she might seem bitter, which was not her way. To ease the harshness of the facts she recast her explanation. "Well, of course, the first seeds were a gift to us as well."

Sarah looked surprised, "What do you mean?"

"Do you know how my ancestors first came to grow corn, which we called maize?"

Aware that she was about to hear one of Mollyockett's famous stories, Sarah made herself comfortable by the old woman's side. "No, I don't know, Mollyockett. Please tell me."

Mollyockett closed her eyes and began quietly, "Long, long ago when the Indians first came to this land, their life was difficult. They lived very much like the animals, picking berries when they were ripe and relying on roots and nuts when there were no berries. One Indian lived apart from the others, and although he foraged for long hours his stomach was never full. The roots and bark he ate tasted foul and stringy. He despaired and prayed to the Great Spirit to take his life quickly instead of starving him to death. As he lay in a field exhausted and hungry, he noticed a beautiful woman with long golden hair walking toward him across the field. Now he had never seen such a beautiful woman, certainly not one with yellow hair, so he wondered what this might mean.

"The woman spoke gently, in a voice like the wind blowing through a field of waving grain. She said, 'The Great Spirit has sent me to ease your pain. But you must honor Him by doing exactly as I say.' The Indian agreed that he would. She instructed him to gather a small pile of dry grass. He did so. Then she told him to rub two sticks together to make a spark over the grass. He did so. When a small fire had flared up, she told him to take the fire and light the entire field to burn away the grass. He did so. As the fire died out and the field was in ashes, the sun began to set. She said, 'Now you must take me by my golden hair and drag me back and forth across the field. As you do this, I will slowly disappear. Do not be troubled. I will never leave you.'

"The Indian feared to do as she said, but feared more to disobey her. He followed her instructions exactly. Sure enough, as he dragged her back and forth across the field, she slowly disappeared. When she was altogether gone, he fell asleep weeping for the loss of the beautiful messenger. He slept a long sleep. When he awoke, he looked over the field. Green grass-like plants grew everywhere he had dragged the golden-haired messenger. Weeks went by. Soon, as he tended the field, he saw that each plant had produced a fruit with yellow seeds. Fine golden hair, just like the hair of the maiden, covered the seeds. He remembered her promise, never to leave him. From that day, we have always grown corn. When the hair covering the kernels within the husk is golden, we harvest it. And as long as we do as the messenger of the Great Spirit advised us, we will never be hungry."

Sarah smiled. "What a good story, Mollyockett. Do you believe it is true?"

Mollyockett chuckled. "What I believe does not matter. I know we have corn and I know it is a gift. We must always be grateful for the gifts of nature and treat them with respect. Even when I gathered berries, I did not strip the bushes, but left some for the birds and bears and some to drop to the ground to make new bushes."

Sarah could see the wisdom in this, but wondered if she could leave berries unpicked. She would think about it.

Mollyockett smiled to herself. "I can tell you another story of corn that I know is true—something that really happened to me. In my life I traveled many times from settlements like Fryeburg, Canton Point, Paris, Bethel and Andover, and north to Odanak to carry out religious duties, trade and visit friends. As I set out on one trip, I promised Colonel Mc Mullan of Conway that I would bring him back some special corn seeds. This corn was well suited to a short growing season. I did trade for the seeds and carried the sack by land, lake and river, finally reaching the outskirts of Conway. Before delivering the corn to Colonel Mc Mullan, I decided to pay a visit to my friend, Squire Richard Eastman, who lived on the way to the Colonel's house. Instead of lugging the sack down the long road to Squire Eastman's home and back, I set it on some logs, intending to pick it up on the way back.

"When I returned, the corn, sack and all, had disappeared. I was fit to be tied. I had to go to the Colonel's empty-handed and tell him I had failed to bring his corn. I later found out that a young busybody named Lydia Fisher saw the sack lying on the logs. She figured that the sack was headed to Noah Eastman's mill. So was she. She picked up the sack and took it to Noah, telling him to grind it and that the person who left it would probably come along soon to claim his flour."

Sarah thought to herself of the rhyme she and her friends chanted
to rope games at recess in the schoolyard:

> "Mollyockett lost her pocket.
> Lydia Fisher found it.
> Lydia took it to the mill
> And Uncle Noah ground it."

Now she knew the story behind the rhyme. Sarah decided not to
tell Mollyockett. She might be offended to be the subject of such a
silly verse. Mollyockett folded her arms across her chest still indig-
nant about the wrongly ground corn. "Can you imagine how upset
I was?" Sarah stifled a giggle. Mollyockett noticed and laughed herself. "I suppose it is funny now, but it was not funny then!"

Realizing that the corn stories were over, but wanting Mollyockett
to continue telling of her life, Sarah asked, "What about your baby?
Was it a boy or a girl?"

Mollyockett sighed. "It was a boy. After a short labor, my first
child was born, but he was not living." Mollyockett did not notice
Sarah's expression of sorrow. She went on with her story. "He looked
like he was only asleep and would wake up, but he did not. A great
sadness filled my heart and I thought I would never smile again. The
priest anointed him with holy oil. He consoled us, saying that the
baby was sinless and was in the arms of God already. After we buried
the baby, Piol and I tried to bury our sorrow and continue our lives.
Blessedly, I was soon with child again. I worried and prayed everyday for a healthy baby and my prayers were answered." Sarah was
relieved. "God is good," she said. "You must have been very happy."

"I was," Mollyockett replied. "Marie Marguerite, my first living
child, was truly another gift. I remained healthy and strong throughout my term. While I waited for her birth I made tiny new clothes
and blankets, and decorated a bundling board with a design of quills
and deerskin fringe. She was born in the women's house in late
spring with the help of Piol's aunts and my friend, Marie Marguerite

Marie Marguerite's Baptismal Certificate

Mollyockett's first living child, fathered by Piol Susup, was baptized at the mission church at Odanak on May 31, 1764. A copy of the Record of Baptisms, Marriages and Deaths is kept at the church of St. Francis-du-Lac. The original is in the Archives du Seminaire de Nicolet near Quebec.

Salier. I had chewed on partridge berries at the first pain and so the birth was easy. Baby Marie was a good looking child with honey colored skin and chestnut eyes. The women exclaimed about her beauty. I smiled at my dear friend and said, 'I hope she is as good and kind as you are. I will give her your name and I ask you to be her godmother.' Marie Marguerite flushed with pleasure for it was an honor to be selected as spiritual mother for a child. Piol chose his friend, Jean Baptiste, to be our baby's godfather.

"I laid little Marie Marguerite in a bed of cattail, milkweed fluff, feathers and moss I had gathered throughout the season. This soft nest prevented chafing and also absorbed wetness. When I moved back to the wigwam, Piol was proud and happy. He loved Marie Marguerite for herself, but also because she helped to replace the children he had lost. Because, as I have told you, the letter "r" is difficult for most Abenakis to say, we called her Molly Susup, so really she had my name and Piol's. At the end of May on a beautiful sunny day we took little Molly to the church. As I held her in my arms, the priest read the rite of baptism and made the sign of the cross on her forehead with holy water. Her arms flew back in surprise because the water was cold, but she did not cry. We took this as a good sign.

"Then after the sacrament, as we watched, the priest recorded her name and ours in a large bound book, *The Registry of Baptisms, Marriages and Deaths*. I asked Father to tell us what he had written. He lifted the book as if it were a holy text and held it in both hands. In a solemn voice he usually saved for the Mass, he read, 'In the Year 1764, on the 31st of May, our cure baptised Marie Marguerite, born the 29th of April of the legitimate marriage of Pierre Joseph and Marie Agathe, Abenaki savages.' Sarah looked shocked and upset as Mollockett continued to quote from the Registry. 'The godfather is Jean Baptiste Cartier and the godmother, Marie Marguerite Salier.'"

"Savages?" whispered Sarah. Surely no one who knew her would call Mollyockett a savage!

Noticing Sarah's discomfort, Mollyockett explained, "Sarah, the priest meant no dishonor by calling us savages. That was just the word they used to mean 'native Indian.' When he had finished he closed the book. He held his hand over us in benediction. 'Well, good people, little Marie's baptism is now recorded in the official registry of the Church of St. Francis-du-Lac. God bless her and protect her. God bless her parents and godparents as they raise this precious child. Go in peace.'

"I soon returned to my work in the fields and at home, carrying Molly with me in her colorful bundling board on my back. Piol did not want to leave us for a while, but before long he once again joined Jean Baptiste and the other men on hunting trips. We lived well and enjoyed watching little Molly grow into an active, good natured child.

"In her second winter, Piol was late in returning from a moose hunt. After the sun had set, a bitter night wind began to howl. Soon I heard men's voices approaching. I could tell something was wrong. They carried Piol into the long house. He was covered with ice and nearly frozen to death." Sarah gasped at this shocking turn of events, but Mollyockett went on, unnoticing. "The hunters had located a moose, and chased it to a place where they hoped to encircle it and move in for the kill. The moose, his nostrils flaring and eyes wide with fear, fled awkwardly through deep snow drifts and out onto the ice covering a deep pond. The men told me that Piol led the charge and as he approached the moose, shaggy with its winter coat, the ice broke through and both the animal and Piol were plunged into the freezing water. Each time Piol tried to pull himself out, the ice broke off. His companions found a fallen sapling and cut it loose from the frozen snow bank. They extended it across the ice. Piol had enough strength left to grab hold and they pulled him across the ice to safety. Meanwhile the moose forced his way through the ice till he was on solid ground, then climbed up onto the shore and reentered the woods without looking back.

"The men scarcely noticed the moose lumbering off. They gathered around Piol as he lay on the ground, dripping freezing water that quickly encrusted him with ice. He was numb with cold and breathing shallowly. Jean Baptiste scraped off as much ice as he could. Another friend removed his own robe and covered Piol. Two men wrapped his arms around their shoulders and carried him for hours back to the village, bringing him directly to our fire.

"I could see that he was in bad shape. I prayed for his recovery as I built up the fire and brewed hot medicine. I removed his wet clothing and rubbed his limbs with balsam salve which I knew to cure frostbite. I rubbed his chest with rough bark till it was red and raw and applied a poultice of the bruised root of Solomon seal and the inner bark of wild cherry. Members of his family continuously rubbed the salve into his arms and into his mouth. He shuddered violently and his teeth clenched. I had to pry them apart to doctor him.

"After several hours, the shuddering diminished, but the cold was replaced with a fever. He threw off his covers and talked crazily in a rasping voice. He urged the hunters to follow the moose. He talked to his first wife and wept for his lost children. I made poultices of steeped moosewood bark and applied them to his chest to relieve congestion. I fed him clover tea tonic hoping to bring down his fever, still he grew hotter and lost consciousness.

"Fearing the worst, I asked Uncle Lucien to fetch one of the priests. The priest who had baptised Molly came at once, carrying a satchel containing the holy elements. He took one look at Piol and began the rite of Holy Unction, putting the sanctified oil on Piol's lids. As if he heard the prayers, Piol opened his eyes. He looked at the group of relatives and friends surrounding him and then at the priest. He understood the end was near.

"I knelt at his head and he shifted so he could see my face. He seemed to be peering through a fog. I am sure he smiled. Then he said, ' My wife, I am sorry to leave you. Take care of little Molly and tell her always that I loved her. Pray for my soul.' Then he closed his eyes forever.

"We prepared Piol's body for burial in the spring, when the ground thawed. Later that day, I went out into the cold air to the shores of the nearby pond. I was crying inside, mourning for my husband. I walked out onto the frozen pond. The ice was thick. How could Piol have fallen through in such a place? Suddenly a deep moaning rose from beneath me. It rumbled away. Then all was still. I was frightened. My heart raced and I stopped breathing. Was this a warning or a message of some kind? The ice moaned again. Nature was mourning with me. I decided that Piol's spirit had spoken to me. It was his way of saying that he would always be with me wherever I went. Comforted, I returned to my family to find out what new path God had chosen for me."

Sarah's eyes glistened with tears. What could she say? She took the old woman's hand and sat quietly holding it.

After a time, Mollyockett continued. "Well, that was long ago, but I treasure my time with Piol and still think of him. Another day I will tell you how I honored his memory and retrieved his soul from Purgatory. But now I will rest awhile."

Sarah waited until she was certain Mollyockett was asleep. Then she quietly gathered up the breakfast remains and returned home.

Chapter 8

As she approached Mollyockett's wigwam, Sarah stumbled over a root. Her mind was not on the path, but on her elderly patient. What sadness Mollyockett had known. By the time she was thirty, she had lost her mother, father, sister, husband and many friends and relatives. Nevertheless, here she was, a wise, clever, old woman, still alive, though probably not for long. Sarah wondered if it was wrong to hope that Mollyockett would continue to be willing to use her dwindling strength telling stories. Sarah's concern evaporated when she entered the wigwam and saw that Mollyockett had propped herself up against a rolled blanket. She had smoothed her hair. Smiling, Mollyockett turned her dim eyes toward Sarah as she entered.

"Dear child," Mollyockett said, "I have been looking forward to your visit. I am a little hungry this afternoon. Have you brought me something tasty?"

"Well, I do have corn bread and cheese and a slice of grandmother's blueberry pie." Sarah set the basket beside the pallet and removed the homespun cloth that covered Mollyockett's lunch.

Mollyockett nodded with satisfaction. "That sounds mighty good." She nibbled a wedge of cheddar and asked, "Are you interested in hearing more of my story?"

"Oh, yes," Sarah said eagerly, "I was afraid to ask. I don't want to tire you out."

Mollyockett blinked her eyes and raised herself a little on the pillow behind her. " I think I'm feeling pretty well today. Now, let's see. Where was I?" Mollyockett chewed thoughtfully on her cornbread. "I told you how I lost Piol and was left with little Molly. Piol did not know when he passed on to the spirit world that he was father to a second child. Sometimes I think that Piol's soul moved into the child within me. I knew that the baby would be a boy. Sure enough, seven months later as the swamp maple leaves were turning a fiery red, my son was born. I named him Piol Susup, for his father. He was a sturdy little boy with straight black hair that stood up all over his head. As a pet name we called him 'Apsokil Matuwehs', 'Little Porcupine.' His bright black eyes followed me everywhere as I moved about the wigwam, tending Molly or preparing cornbread. When I went into the fields to harvest pumpkins, I used the same backboard worked with quills and beads I had made for Molly. He slept soundly most of the time he was outdoors, but fussed more when he was inside the wigwam. 'Just like his father,' I thought. 'He loves to be under the open sky. He'll be a hunter.'

"As the winter wore on I grew restless. Although the children kept me busy, I had a deep longing to visit what I still considered my home, the Pequawket territory on the shores of the Saco River where I had lived with my family as a girl. The English, after a series of fierce battles at northern forts, had defeated the French. The French king gave up the northern territory to the English king. Some French people returned across the sea to their homeland, but others remained. Now the few remaining Indian warriors were of little interest to either side. Some settled into the peaceful life they had always preferred or found other ways to make themselves useful to the English.

"Other Indian warriors felt betrayed and took vengeance on anyone in their path. Luckily these angry ones were few and the white men many, so these Indians lived as renegades and did not do much harm. When the ice had just left the ponds, I learned that a small party of my neighbors, led by Captain Swassin, an old chief, planned to return to their homelands along the rivers of Maine. I decided to join them.

"We traveled south by canoe and by foot along the old routes. Luckily we suffered no misfortunes. We stopped along the way at Andover, Sudbury Canada and Canton Point to visit with settlers we knew and with the few Abenaki families remaining in the region. By the time the oak leaves were as big as a mouse's ear, we were approaching Fryeburg. I was amazed. The ridge of pine trees that had been knee high when I left now towered overhead. What had once been the hoeing place of my family was inhabited by a settlement of English people. I learned that someone in Boston had granted Pequawket land to Colonel Frye so he could build a settlement there. I was upset, but kept my anger to myself. It would do no good.

"On the first nights after our arrival, the settlers obeyed the customs of hospitality and invited us to stay in their homes. Our band settled in or near several households in the way we would in a kinsman's wigwam. Some of our party stayed with Nathaniel Smith and his wife, Betty, at their home near the mill. Others stayed with the Osgoods, the Merrills, the Swans and Moses Ames' family. We stowed our belongings where we could and at evening rolled out our sleeping robes and slept in sheds or barns or on the floor, often eight or ten to a room. We shared what provisions we had and accepted what the settlers offered us. Since it was spring, the corn porridge was sweetened with thickened maple sap. They also served donuts fried in moose suet and bear grease. One night we had a treat, broiled beaver tail. It was fat and juicy. Boiled bracken roots made a tasty green." Sarah tried not to show her distaste for this "feast." Beaver tail and bracken, Yuck!

Unaware of Sarah's repugnance, Mollyockett continued, "Although the white settlers were kind at first, it became clear that our welcome was beginning to wear thin. They were not used to our ways, and seemed annoyed when we spoke among ourselves in our own language and more so when we spoke French.

"One of the band who had moved south with us, was a respected hunter and guide named Sabattis. You remember I told you of a youth who was carried away from Odanak by Rogers' soldiers?" Sarah nodded. Mollyockett continued, "Well, this is the same Sabattis, now grown to manhood. As part of a treaty, he had been exchanged for white prisoners. After several years traveling in Maine he returned to our village on the St. Francis River. When Piol was alive I hardly noticed Sabattis, but on the trip to Fryeburg we became well acquainted.

"Like Piol, Sabattis was a skilled woodsman. When he hunted, he always brought back plentiful game. When he fished, the salmon seemed to leap out of the water. He was able to carry heavy burdens for many hours without tiring. Unlike Piol, Sabattis was younger than I. He was very handsome."

Sarah's interest intensified at the mention of a handsome young man. "It sounds like you were interested in him. Tell me what he was like!"

Mollyockett shut her eyes as if to conjure up an image of this person from her past. "He was tall," she began, "and moved through the forest with long, graceful strides. His clothing fit tighter than most, because of the fullness of his muscles. He was broad of shoulder, but his waist was narrow. He was proud of his manliness and was a bit of a show-off. One spring the river began to thaw. We were still wearing our winter leggings, but he plunged into the water frolicking among the slabs of ice. When he climbed back onto the bank, he acted refreshed, as after a swim on a hot summer day.

"His face was as good to look at as any I have seen, firm but smiling lips, high cheekbones, and dark, warm eyes the color of chestnuts. His hair was shiny and black. He wore it pulled back in a braid, but often wrapped a beaded thong around his forehead. The eyes of women followed him always. They could not help it. Everywhere he went the women whispered to each other, 'Wolapewiw!' which means 'He is handsome!' Others whispered behind their hands and referred to him as 'mascap.'"

Sarah interrupted. "Another Indian word, 'mascap.' What does it mean?"

Mollyockett flushed beneath her pallor. "I should not have said that. You are too young for such things."

"Mollyockett, please tell me. I'm grown-up enough," Sarah pleaded.

"Well, dear, please don't tell your relatives I spoke like this to you, but it means, let's see, something like 'over-sexed man.'"

Sarah blushed, but tried to look composed. "Oh, I understand." She wasn't sure she did, but she promised herself to find out.

Mollyockett smiled wistfully and continued her story. "I, too, watched him carefully, as if he were a bold stag running fearlessly through the forest or an eagle soaring above. When he looked at me, I shivered even though the sun was warm. My heart pounded, my cheeks flushed. I found myself wanting to talk to him, but not sure what to say. I remembered my hours in the sandy dunes of Plymouth with Hadomit so many years before. It was the same feeling only more powerful. Sometimes I felt ashamed. Here I was a grown woman, the widow of a good man, the mother of small children. Such feelings were not proper. Still my interest did not shrink, but instead grew faster than a pumpkin vine in the heat of midsummer.

"Before long, as we traveled south to Fryeburg, Sabattis began to sit next to me at the fire. He brought wood and stacked it neatly nearby, although usually that was the work of women or children. He carved a doll for Molly and enjoyed watching her play with it. I began to sense his eyes on me in a way I had not known before, almost burning, as if he could read my thoughts and see into my heart. I began to hope he could not read my mind to know the confusion and wild emotions that occupied my thoughts. Then at other times I hoped he did know how I felt, because I could never tell him.

"Shortly after our arrival in Fryeburg, I felt uncomfortable in the

Swan's crowded cabin. I settled the children in their robes, asked someone to keep an eye on them for a while, and left for a walk as the sun began to set. Sabattis was also staying with the Swan family with whom he was acquainted. He, too, decided to walk in the evening air. We met, as if by chance, and he asked if he could join me. I nodded without emotion, while my inner voice said, 'Yes, yes, yes!' We walked for a while discussing the need either to move on or to build our own wigwams before the settlers tired of our company. Then we sat for a while beside the river enjoying the rose and golden colors of the setting sun.

"First Sabattis talked of little things that I have forgotten. After a while, he said he intended to set up a wigwam on land adjoining the Swan homestead starting the next day. He asked if I would share it. I was surprised, but pleased to know that he wanted my company. I thought a bit, then replied that this might be a good idea, but to avoid gossip we would need to find others to stay, as well.

"He laughed, 'Molly, you misunderstand me. I am asking you and the children to be my family. I want to live with you forever.'

Sarah sighed. "How beautiful. The man you loved proposing! And at sunset. You must have been so excited. What did you say?"

"Yes, I was pleased and happy but also worried. I was a believer in the Catholic faith and far from the nearest priests. When I was a child, we often traveled from Canton Point to Norridgewock to visit a priest who ministered to Indians there. He was long gone, chased off by the English. How could we properly marry? Also, although I prayed for Piol very often, I still believed that his soul might linger in Purgatory, so I was concerned about that as well. How could I take a new husband while my first husband did not yet rest easy? Sabattis saw my hesitation and asked to know my thoughts. I told him my concerns.

"He was still for a while. Then he said, 'These are honest thoughts and worthy of the good woman I know you to be. Here is what my heart tells me. As to the distance from priests, I believe that when God decides that two people should be together he stirs them so

Birchbark Wigwam

The grounds of the Abenaki Museum at Odanak contain wigwams constructed using ancient techniques. Mollyockett probably lived in such a dwelling.

(Photo by the author)

they cannot be apart. I feel such a stirring and I think you do, too. If living as husband and wife is what God wants, we should obey.'

"He paused to see if I objected. Since I remained quiet, he continued. 'Also, Molly, we should remember the old ways of our people. From the beginning of time, when the desire to be together moved in their hearts, a man and a woman pledged to each other and asked for the help of the Great Spirit who made the world. I believe the Great Spirit and God are one. We will make a sacred promise together in the name of the Great Spirit. When we get the chance to travel to a priest, we will be married in the eyes of the Church. Meanwhile we will already be married in the eyes of God. As to your dead husband, your loyalty honors both him and you. I have been taught that freedom from Purgatory can be purchased by giving a gift to the Church. You can begin setting aside coins, and when you have enough, we will travel north together, be married by a priest and redeem Piol's soul. Meanwhile we should do as God directs us and live together as parents of your children and as loving partners in life.'"

"That sounds sensible to me," Sarah mused. Silently, she wondered what the church elders and Reverend Strickland would say. "But, what did you decide?"

"I agreed. Within three days we moved into Sabattis' new wigwam, although we continued to take many of our meals with the Swans. Each night after supper we settled into our own wigwam. I looked forward to the darkness and enjoyed his embraces. I felt toward him something far more powerful than the sense of affectionate duty I had shared with Piol. Together we were more than just children of nature. At times we seemed to be the life force itself. Until then I could not have believed that such powerful feelings were possible. In the Bible, Jesus says the most important things in life are Faith, Hope and Love, but the greatest of these is Love. During these early days and nights together with Sabattis as my husband, I knew this to be true.

"We were very happy and in less than a year we were blessed with a child, a handsome girl we named Ursula. Little Molly was now four years old and although she ignored her brother, she loved her little sister and played with her like a doll, rearranging her clothes, showing her bright leaves and chattering. Later Molly loved to feed Ursula cornmeal and berries, and sang silly songs to make the baby laugh."

Sarah furrowed her brow. "Mollyockett, you and Sabattis had no farm. How did you feed three children? And how did Sabattis ever think you could earn money to give to the Church?"

Mollyockett responded thoughtfully, "Jesus says that we should be like the lilies of the field who just grow without concern. We were like that. God provided what we needed. As I told you, Sabattis was a fine hunter, so we were never without meat. But more important than a strong arm and a steady eye, Sabattis was a clear thinker with a good memory. During the time of his captivity he had learned English, and spoke easily in that tongue as well as French and several Indian languages. He also had a pleasing manner with other people. Some years before, he and his friend, Natanis, had guided General Benedict Arnold to a battle in Quebec. Some of the settlers, including Mr. Nathaniel Merrill, had come to trust him as a guide. He would lead them on hunts or help them scout out places for new farmsteads or settlements. For these services he was paid. And, of course, he hunted and trapped for himself along the way and always returned from trips with a new supply of pelts. During this time in Fryeburg and later in Bethel, we lived close by the Swan family. We helped them and they helped us.

"Although you might think my time would be filled with caring for the children and preparing food and clothing, I was strong and restless and soon began again to gather herbs to make medicines. The settlers began to call on me as a healer and a midwife and paid me for this in various ways. Also I made baskets and other useful articles. People found my designs pleasing and I could easily sell or trade any article I made. In good weather I laid out a trap line along the water's edge and caught many beavers. The white settlers valued these above other furs and paid well for them. The number of coins in my pouch grew steadily."

Sarah's eyes were wide. She had never met a woman who earned money. The women of Andover worked hard day in, day out, but if money ever changed hands it was the men who were responsible. Women did barter eggs or butter, or woven goods for other supplies they needed or made purchases with money their husband had earned selling animals or ploughing another's fields, but they seldom had money of their own. She wondered what James would think of a wife who earned her own living. "I don't see why I shouldn't have some way to earn my own money," she mused. "If Mollyockett could do it, I can too." She resolved to think harder and more practically about her future rather than just letting her life take its course after the pattern of her mother and aunts and grandmother, as good and loyal as they were.

As Sarah considered Mollyockett's example, the old woman was lost in her own recollections. She could not tell Sarah how Sabattis' body felt against hers under the fur robe, how he had held her and caressed her. How she had nibbled at his ear and run her hands all over his body. How she had eagerly welcomed him into her and held him tight while the world outside their passion faded till there was nothing left but two hearts pounding, lips seeking and an indescribable rush of passionate release. She would never, never forget how she had loved him in those early years, despite what was to follow.

Both women, the very young and the very old, emerged from their musings simultaneously. They looked at each other wondering whether their expressions betrayed their thoughts. Mollyockett smiled, "Well, where was I? My mind seems to have wandered off like a cloud on a windy day."

Sarah smiled, too. "I was day dreaming, also, I guess. Your stories make me wonder what my life will be like—how I wish it to be, how I can make my wishes real."

Mollyockett nodded. "These are important thoughts for a young person. It is tempting to take the easy path and do always what others expect. But I have found that the harder path, the path that overcomes difficulties and challenges your strength and ability can be most satisfying. You come to trust yourself."

"Molly," exclaimed Sarah, "you were like Cinderella!" "Cinderella?" said Mollyockett. "Who is Cinderella? This is no name I know."

Pleased to be able to tell Mollyockett a story, Sarah said, "Cinderella was a beautiful girl living a hard life who met a handsome prince, fell in love, married him, became a princess and lived happily ever after!"

"Well, dear," said Mollyockett, "that is an interesting story, but mine is a little different. I was a princess to begin with. The lands we are on and for many miles around were once my kingdom. I did marry a handsome prince, but as for happily ever after, you will have to judge for yourself when I tell you what happened. But that's for another day. I think I need to sleep a while." As she spoke, her eyes were already closing.

Sarah stood a moment looking fondly at the sleeping old woman. Then she left to begin the list of chores Aunt Sophia had planned for her. Laundry, cooking, weeding, watching the baby. Maybe she should ask Uncle Thomas to teach her to shoot his rifle. Maybe she should learn more about herbs and medicines. Maybe....

Chapter 9

The Sabbath was cold and rainy. The ferns along the path, struck by frost, were already brown and beaten down by the weather. Sarah clutched her cape around her as she rushed to take Mollyockett her breakfast. She did not want to be late for church. Her parents were eager to hear the visiting preacher from Buxton. People said that his persuasive preaching inspired the baptism of many settlers. Of course, it was also a chance to see James and allow him to see her in her best dress and bonnet. After laying out biscuits and pouring tea, Sarah told Mollyockett that she would return after church to deliver her midday meal. She hoped Mollyockett would continue the romantic story that had intrigued her the day before.

When Sarah returned shortly before noon, Mollyockett was eager to find out what the preacher had said. "Molly, he was very exciting to listen to. He speaks beautifully about the joys of being a child of God and a follower of Jesus, and not so much about the terrible torments due sinners or those outside the church. Uncle Thomas says the preacher was educated at Harvard College in Cambridge. He has learned Greek and Latin and knows all about things that happened thousands of years ago. Aunt Sophia says what's more important is that he has studied the Bible, each line and verse, and can quote long passages, whole chapters, from memory. I liked his deep voice and the way he looked at every person, as if he was speaking to each one alone. I know he spoke to me, and I promised myself to be a better person from now on."

Mollyockett smiled, "Well, dear, I will watch for improvement, but it seems to me that you are already a good girl. You have certainly been kind to me, and I do thank you." Sarah blushed, but her eyes lit up with pleasure. Mollyockett patted her hand. "But tell me more about the preacher. I surely would like to have heard him. I always enjoyed listening to the preachers, especially the Methodists. Of course, when I was at St. Francis du Lac, I attended Mass every week. But when I lived in the towns around here, I visited the Methodist and Congregational churches to learn what the settlers said about the ways of God. Sometimes I was not sure that Indians were welcome to sit in the benches with the white folks. When that was so, I often pulled a log in from outside and set it up at the back of the church right in the center aisle so I would not miss a word."

Sarah was surprised. "Did you ever go to church here in Andover?"

"Mollyockett smiled, "Yes, I did, and here I was made welcome. Most church people, especially the women, treated me with friendship and respect. We talked together in order to learn more about God and how to live according to His word. I have always thought that church people, especially the Methodists in Bethel were dreadfully clever folks. They could discuss the Gospel and figure out what it meant for them in their daily lives. They used the Church's teaching to become better people themselves, not to lord it over others.

"I always tried to do right, but I know that sometimes my idea of right did not match that of my white neighbors. Once, some years after I had left Fryeburg and was living in Bethel, I took some blueberries in one of my baskets to Mrs. Chapman, the minister's wife, early on a Monday morning. She was a cool woman, full of starch, but I counted her and her husband as friends. She noticed the berries were very fresh and asked when I had picked them. I told her I had found a large clump of highbush berries the day before as I walked in the sunshine along the river. She chastised me for picking on the Sabbath. I set the berries on the table without a word and left the house. I was puzzled at first and then quite angry. Hadn't God placed the berries there on my way through the woods on a beautiful summer day? Hadn't I picked them as a gift for a friend? How could it be evil to pick them? My mind worked on that for some time.

"A few days later I returned to the Chapman's house. I was still upset. Mrs. Chapman laid me a place at the table as she usually did. I refused to eat and said what I thought about the blueberries. I told her that the God I loved would not begrudge me a basket of blueberries, especially since they were a gift for her! Jesus said, 'It is more blessed to give than to receive.' She seemed taken aback. Perhaps she was surprised that I was as concerned about God's will as she was. She said she was sorry she had spoken so harshly. She said my ways were different from hers but I was no less a Christian woman and she would remember that in the future. Again she offered food, corn cooked in syrup, moose steak and blueberry cake, if I recall. I agreed to eat at her table and it tasted good." Mollyockett smiled with satisfaction at this recollection.

Sarah wondered how to change the subject from church and blueberries to Mollyockett's life with her handsome husband. She brushed her fine blond hair back behind her ears and tried a question that she hoped wasn't too bold. "What was life for your family like in Fryeburg in the early days?"

"Well," Mollyockett began, "I was very much amazed at how Pequawket had changed in a few years from an Indian village into a growing English settlement. This, I learned, was largely due to the cleverness and hard work of Colonel Joseph Frye. The colonial government had given him a large tract of land to build a town. It seemed strange to me that people in Boston could give the land that belonged to my people to any person for any reason, but that is what happened. Colonel Frye and others were given Indian land as payment for the service of their fathers years ago in the wars against the French and the Indians. How could this be? Neither my father nor my grandfather, both great chiefs of our people, signed treaties selling our land, as some other tribes had done."

With increasing animation, Mollyockett continued. "This country, the forests, the lakes and the mighty rivers full of trout and salmon still belonged to us. Yet we were treated like trespassers on land that had been my cradleboard. All the best parcels were already claimed and dotted with farmsteads and mills. Most of us moved onto the land of white families, like poor relations. Some camped on less desirable, uninhabited land outside the main settlement.

"I did not blame Colonel Frye for building on our land. He only took what he believed was legally granted him. But I know who the true owners are." She crossed her arms on her chest and nodded sternly. Then her face softened as she resumed the tale.

"Colonel Frye was an able man. He and his wife, Mehitable, were hard-working, Godly people. He led the first white families through some difficult times. Mehitable, as I recall, was a Poor and maybe is related to the Poors who live here in Andover. They are good people, too.

"White men," she mused, "seem to need more things to make their lives suitable than Indians do. When the first settlers arrived they brought guns, metal frying pans and kettles, various lighting devices—things we were amazed at. How could they need more? We carried few belongings with us and made, hunted or grew everything we required.

"The white men were not satisfied with what they had carried in with them but were always going off on long trips to bring back more. They often traveled by bateau from Fryeburg to Saco, even in winter. One Thanksgiving, I heard, a small band of men set out for Concord for who knows what supplies. They were delayed by a deep snow and returned more dead than alive. They had walked the seventy miles on snowshoes pulling the goods they felt they needed, more than four hundred pounds of it, on sleds. The hauling ropes wore the skin right off their bones."

Sarah looked curious. "What did they carry back that was so important?"

"Let me think," recollected Mollyockett. "Let's see. Oh, yes. They brought grain and salted meat to help carry us through the winter, of course, and that was welcome. But they also brought all kinds of tools and implements. Most settlers had few tools and prided themselves on what they could do with those few. I heard one man say, 'Give me an axe and I'll make a pianer.' I wasn't sure what a 'pianer' was, but I figured it must be something grand. Colonel Frye was a big one for tools, and seemed to have at least one of everything, a crosscut saw, a hand saw, a hack saw, several hammers, a broadax, a hatchet, broad and narrow chisels, a breaking up plough, hoes, shovels and augers of sundry sizes and many others I can't name. He could never in his lifetime use all he had, but he treasured these tools. Though he willingly shared with his neighbors, he kept a book that recorded every item loaned, when it was expected back and when it was returned. He treated his tools like children." She chuckled, "His record book was like the book the priests kept to write down the baptisms, marriages and deaths. It was a holy book, for him."

Sarah smiled. "I know some people who are like that. Some of them treat their belongings better than they treat people."

Mollyockett wondered if maybe she had been too critical. She added hastily, "To be fair, Mr. Frye's tools were always in use by someone as the settlers built barns, sheds, schools, churches, mills, bridges, town roads and eventually a road from Fryeburg to Falmouth.

"The year we arrived in Fryeburg, Colonel Frye was just building a new home on the hill in the center of town. We thought it was remarkable. It was a two storied building with a roof like this." Mollyockett formed a gambrel shape with her hands. "It seemed very large to us, about twelve paces wide and twenty paces long, with a big barn attached at the rear. He and his wife eventually had nine children. Still, why did they need so much room? Sabattis and

I often with Molly, John, Ursula and sometimes with Baseel, a young man who sometimes visited, lived in our one room wigwam with no difficulty.

"The ways of the settlers often surprised us and we watched them with interest to see what we could learn. More and more we became familiar with their customs and found that we could live better if we helped them and became their friends. As time went by, I grew uncomfortable with the rough and violent ways of some Indians, and made more and more friends among the white people. Very soon the settlers came to Sabattis to get his advice on the best way to reach a destination or later on the location of roads. He was familiar with the Indian trails, which always provided the easiest route.

"I resumed my gathering of herbs and prepared medicines to heal the sick. Now, I remembered well that Mr. John Evans, the hunter who lived nearby, was the same man I had seen with Major Rogers during the massacre at Odanak. But I also remembered that he had tried to show mercy toward my little cousin, so I forgave him. When he told me that Mrs. Evans' hand was badly infected I offered to cure it. I climbed up to the top of Jockey Cap where the arched fronds of Solomon seal grew in thick clumps. I dug up the roots. These I ground into a paste and applied as a poultice. The swelling went down in a day and the redness was entirely gone within a week. Mr. and Mrs. Evans were most grateful. They told others of my cure. Soon many settlers sought my aid. As more women moved to the village from Massachusetts or other settlements to join their husbands, I was often called to help women in childbirth or to soothe colicky babies.

"In this manner we made ourselves useful to the settlers and were always welcome at their tables. We pretty much kept to ourselves, but paid attention to what our neighbors were doing so as not to miss an opportunity to trade furs or medicine or other handwork for coins or for goods they did not need. As a reward for helping her through the delivery of a healthy boy, Mrs. Osgood gave me her second best iron kettle, which I used for many years to brew bark and herbal teas."

"Did you always live in town?" Sarah asked.

"Well," Mollyockett replied, "most of the time I lived with the settlers, but sometimes, especially after Sabattis was gone, I went off alone or with a group of Indians."

Sarah started. "After Sabattis was gone," she thought. "What does that mean?"

Mollyockett, unaware of Sarah's dismay, continued. "The group I often traveled with was made up of Indians from several tribes, but we hunted, fished and planted together as one people. Captain Swassin was designated sagamore, for he had served the English against the French and had earned their respect and a military title. When we had matters to resolve with the settlers, Captain Swassin often spoke for us. He also resolved disputes within our group. Sometimes when Sabattis had been drinking, he complained that Captain Swassin had not taken his advice or had wrongly settled a matter, but generally we all were glad to have him speak for us. He was wise in some ways, but in others he was as foolish as any man I ever knew.

"Occasionally we moved from Fryeburg to other locations that had been Indian land but were now being settled by white people. One place we visited often was Sudbury Canada, a growing village on the Androscoggin River. This land, too, was given to settlers as a reward for service in the war against the French. In this case, the land was given to a group of proprietors, including Mr. Twitchell. I always told the first settlers of Sudbury Canada, 'I am a rightful proprietor of this town!' But I did not receive any encouragement, much less any land!

"Joseph Twitchell organized the town of Sudbury Canada as Joseph Frye had in Fryeburg. In fact, one of the first settlers came by way of Fryeburg, so there was much commerce between the towns. As I have told you, Sabattis and I often lived with or near our friends, the Swans. James Swan was a clever man and he made good use of Sabattis' knowledge of the woodlands. For my part, I enjoyed the company of his wife. One time to surprise her I made a comforter

Mollyockett's Cave

Mollyockett often camped within the shelter of this cave atop Jockey Cap Ridge, a granite outcropping in Fryeburg, Maine. Mollyockett was born in Fryeburg, then called Pigwacket.

(Photo by the author)

and filled it with the feathers of geese and ducks I had shot. She was mighty pleased with this gift. When the Swan family moved to Sudbury Canada, now called Bethel, we moved with them.

"Just as in Fryeburg, the first settlers, led by Mr. Josiah Richardson, had been given land as a reward for the services of their ancestors in a raid on Canada almost a hundred years before. The colonial government did not have money so they gave letters of credit for our land. How could they do that? I will never understand. It still angers me.

"At first ten men camped on the land and worked together to fell trees, lay out parcels and build camps. Then they returned to their homes in Massachusetts for the winter. The next year they came back and built a sawmill on the falls. They cleared land and planted corn and rye. Three built sturdy houses of split logs, but they left them to return to Massachusetts until the next year, fearing the harshness of the winter.

"The third year some returned bringing others to settle the town. In early spring, Mr. Benjamin Russell brought his wife and daughter, Mary, then a girl about your age, from Fryeburg, a distance of some forty miles. He walked on snowshoes pulling his wife and daughter and supplies on a hand sled. Mrs. Russell told me it took two days. Her daughter was feeling poorly at the time and could barely sit up. Mrs. Russell said both she and her girl tried to walk some of the way, but the snow was too deep and they foundered. They were mighty glad to arrive at Sudbury Canada and thanked God for delivering them out of the wilderness. I thanked God to have another woman nearby, though I also enjoyed many days of hunting with Mr. Russell. The Russell's grandaughter, Martha, became one of my best friends. I taught her how to prepare some herbs and to make dyes. We enjoyed working together and talking. If I were stronger I'd like to do the same with you. You are a lot like Martha.

"I did what I could to get along with the growing number of settlers. Many of these folks admired my handiwork and asked me to make special items. Mr. Eli Twitchell of Sudbury Canada wanted to surprise his wife with a gift to celebrate their anniversary. I agreed to weave a piece of fancy cloth to be made into a purse. I wove a base of heavy cord. As I wove, I twisted in a pattern of stripes, zigzags and diamonds, using moosehair thread dyed red, green, blue and yellow. Some years before, Mr. Twitchell's brother, Simeon, a metalworker, had made a beautiful silver clasp. Mr. Twitchell decided to use this clasp to fasten the purse. Then his sister sewed the purse together cleverly, adding a lining and two inner pockets of flannel. Mrs. Twitchell was mighty pleased and told me many times how much she admired my needlework.

Both Sides of Mollyockett's Purse

The purse combines the construction of a European-style pocketbook, a skillfully woven Algonkian design created from hemp and dyed moosehair, a commercially woven wool lining and a clasp made by Eli Twitchell or perhaps by his brother, a silversmith. The clasp is dated 1778, although Twitchell's daughter, Lucia Kimball, said the purse was made about 1785.

(Photo provided by the Bethel Historical Society and Regional History Center)

"I could see all along that if my family and other Indian families were to survive, we would need to learn and use many of the white men's ways. When I heard that the minister ran a school in his parlor to teach boys and girls to read and write, I asked if my children could go, too. He was a good Christian man and said they would be welcome. So Molly Marguerite first became a student when she was about your age. She was a big, strong girl and loved to play games with the boys. She often beat them in races and throwing games. Still she paid attention in the schoolroom and the minister said she was a quick learner. Soon she was helping him with the younger children. I thought Molly was a good girl, but she had a stubborn streak that caused her to take a wrong path." Mollyockett sighed. "It still pains me to think of it."

Sarah held her breath. What had Molly, this smart, strong, able girl her own age done to cause her mother grief? She waited, then could wait no more. "What happened Mollyockett? Will you tell me what Molly did that upset you? Maybe I can learn a lesson."

"Well, child, I hope you never do what she did. Although she spoke English perfectly and was successful with the settlers, she loved to spend time among the Indians. Soon the leader I told you about, old Captain Swassin, began to pay attention to her. She was good looking. Her dark eyes sparkled and her golden skin was smooth and soft. Her body was more womanly than most girls her age. Swassin was an older man, maybe forty or fifty years old. He asked to marry her. I said 'no.' When I married Piol, he was older than I, but there was not such a big difference. Why should such a beautiful promising girl give herself to such an old bull moose?

"She would not listen and soon I noticed her swelling belly." Sarah was shocked, but tried not to show it. "I scolded her, but there was nothing to do. I still refused her permission to marry Swassin, but I said I would care for her and the child, though she was little more than a child herself. Soon after, the baby, called Molly Piol, was born. She was an agreeable child, but before many years had passed, a coughing disease swept through the settlement

Birch Bark Box Attributed to Mollyockett

This birch bark box is an example of a useful and decorative object using traditional techniques.

(Photo provided by the Bethel Historical Society and Regional History Center)

and my first grandchild departed to join the Great Spirit. As I washed her little body, I wept. She was not to blame for her mother's bad behavior and yet it seemed that she was punished. We buried her in a new burying ground and mourned for a time. But life continues for the survivors of every sadness.

"Before too long, Molly became fond of Joseph Neptune, a Penobscot, who seemed a decent man. He asked to marry her. This time I did not object, although I had my doubts. It was hard to tell what Molly would do from moment to moment. She would be a thoughtful young woman speaking perfect English with the settlers one moment. Then the next she was like a child, refusing to do her chores and telling me to mind my own business. I worried for her future.

"Sure enough, she was not ready to be a wife, and her husband finally could put up with no more foolishness. He left her. I was overcome with shame. Her behavior was not only a stain on her character, but on mine. A grandchild of great Pequawket chiefs should not behave this way. I hung my head for many months. In spite of my sadness, she was my daughter and I did not shun her. Still I know she felt my disappointment and withdrew from me. Soon she moved to Vermont with another group of Abenakis. Some time later she married a white farmer and finally settled down to a responsible life. Vermont is far away and I did not travel there more than once a year, so really I had lost her as well as my grandbaby."

Sarah shook her head in sympathy. "It must have been so sad to lose the baby and then to have your daughter move so far away."

Mollyockett nodded with tears in her eyes. "I still think of that baby and wonder what I should have done to save her. From that time on I worked specially hard to learn how to cure children." She sighed wearily. "Well, that is enough talking for today. Tomorrow I will tell you of my part in what, thankfully, was the last time some of my people with evil in their hearts attacked a settlement and did great damage."

Sarah searched her memory. "I think I've heard about the last Indian raid, but I don't know much. I will be glad to learn more tomorrow. Meanwhile, rest and sleep. Grandma Bragg, Aunt Sophia and some other ladies will come later this afternoon to sit a while. I will see you tomorrow." As she stepped out into the chill, she prayed, "God bless you, poor old soul. Please, Father, keep her comfortable and safe another night."

Chapter 10

"But what about Sabattis?" Sarah wondered as she approached Mollyockett's wigwam. "What did Mollyockett mean when she had said, 'After Sabattis was gone?' How could she bear to part from anyone so handsome and accomplished? How could she leave the father of two of her children?" Sarah had turned these questions over and over in her mind and could find no answers. She was not sure it was polite to ask such personal questions, but when curiosity warred with manners, curiosity usually won. Her mother had often warned her, "Sarah, mind your own business. Curiosity killed the cat." Sarah was never sure what the cat had to do with it. She knew she could not let matters rest. She needed to know how such a romantic relationship had gone wrong.

Sarah pulled open the flap of the wigwam, wondering how she could find out what had become of Sabattis. She was disappointed to see that Mollyockett seemed to be sleeping. She set the basket of food near the sickbed and stirred up the fire, setting a kettle over the flickering logs. As the fire crackled and water on the outside of the kettle sizzled, Mollyockett slowly opened her eyes. She smiled when she saw Sarah nearby. "My dear, you are like a little mouse. I didn't hear you enter. Thank you for bringing—what is it—breakfast or lunch?" She paused in confusion, then gathered her thoughts. "Oh, yes, it's morning. I see the slanted rays of the sun through the door-flap." She considered her condition. She felt no pain, but even lifting her hand required her full concentration. She looked at the basket of food without interest. "I'm not very hungry today, but maybe a little tea would do me good."

Sarah was concerned. Mollyockett wasn't hungry. What did that mean? As frail as she was, the old woman usually had a good appetite. Sarah resolved to tell to tell Aunt Sophia as soon as she returned to the house. Her aunt would know whether loss of appetite was cause for alarm. "Are you feeling well?" she asked. "Is your stomach upset? Do you hurt anywhere?"

The corners of Mollyockett's mouth turned up in a weak attempt to smile. "Don't concern yourself, Sarah. I imagine I'm just a little peaked today. Come sit by me a minute. Just having you near makes me feel better. I forget where we were in my story. Remind me."

"Well," said Sarah hesitantly. "You had just told me about your daughter and her, um, her romances. But, I'm wondering about something else you said."

Mollyockett closed her eyes, slowly like an owl, then opened them again. "Yes, what might that be?"

Sarah paused, then plunged in. "I thought you said you sometimes traveled with other Indian groups, especially after Sabattis was gone. Did you really leave him? How could that happen? I thought you loved him and were happy with him and your babies."

Mollyockett's eyes crinkled with amusement. "What a curious child you are! So you want to know about how my so-called marriage turned from gold to ashes!"

Sarah's face reddened. She was afraid she had gone too far. Maybe Mother was right. Still she wanted to know. "I'm sorry if I've offended you, but I have been wondering what happened. If you don't want to tell me, that's fine. We can talk about something else."

"No, no," said Mollyockett patiently. "It's all right. We are friends now. I will tell you what happened. Raise me a little so I can breathe easier."

Sarah adjusted a blanket to form a pillow and propped Mollyockett against it. She seemed lighter today than yesterday. Mollyockett settled back and ran her hands absently back and forth over the fur rug covering her. "Well, where should I start?" she paused, then began her story.

"I did love Sabattis fiercely and truly. I was proud of his skill in the forest and the respect he earned from the settlers. He enjoyed the children and played with them as if he was a child himself. Most of the time he was all I could want in a husband, but like many men, he often drank too much. Now, I always enjoyed a little rum myself, so I'm not like some who say that liquor is the devil's drink. In fact, in later years, I often found opportunities to visit Dr. Moses Mason's fine house on the main street in Bethel, partly because he usually welcomed me with a cup of rum.

"But Sabattis went beyond a friendly cup of rum now and then. More and more often, settlers would pay him for his help with a jug of liquor, which he was happy to accept. If he drank just a little, he became playful and silly, pretending to be an animal or telling funny stories, acting them out with gestures and faces that made others laugh. When he drank more, he became a different person—rough, angry and unreasonable. At such times he would blame others for slights, real and imagined. He would complain about things he said I had done, or hadn't done, or had done wrong. The venison was tough or undercooked, or overcooked. My herbs and medicines stunk up the place or I should gather more to sell to the settlers. I spent too much, or not enough time at the sickbeds of settlers, or I was helping people he did not like. Once he was taken by drink, there was nothing to do but stay out of the way and wait till he passed out or fell asleep. These unpleasant times happened more and more often.

"In the morning after such a night he would hang his head like a child and promise not to behave so again. Then he would soak his

The Moses Mason House

This early photo shows the home of Dr. Moses Mason on Broad Street in Bethel, Maine. The home now serves as a museum and period house. Mollyockett visited the Masons here on many occasions. The house is operated by the Bethel Historical Society and Regional History Center.

(Photo provided by the Society)

feet in a bucket of cold water, believing that this would lessen the after effects of too much liquor. I do not know where he got the idea that icy feet would cure a headache, but he believed in this remedy. He spent too many mornings freezing his feet. He looked so forlorn, sitting patiently while his toes turned blue. Time after time I believed him and forgave him. At first, I even felt sorry for his sickness in the morning after drinking too much and tried to restore his health with medicines and teas.

"But soon his drunkenness became a habit. He stopped apologizing and instead complained that I would not join him in his pleasure. He said I was too serious, unlike other women he had known. This hurt my feelings, but I kept my temper. This seemed to anger him even more. I kept my problem to myself because I was ashamed. I thought maybe Sabattis was right, maybe I was somehow to blame. So when I saw he had been drinking, whenever possible, I made excuses and took the children with me on an 'urgent' errand.

"After one such time, while he was feeling unusually sorry that he had behaved badly, I reminded him of his promise to return with me to Odanak so we could be married in the church and so I could redeem the soul of my first husband from Purgatory. I said I had saved some money but felt I would not need that. I would take pelts to sell at the trading post. He agreed to my plan in order to satisfy me, but looked uneasy. Later I found out the reason for his discomfort.

"I decided that I would return in style to Odanak the next spring. I would wear my old leggings, woolen dress, mantle and moccasins as I traveled. But once I arrived at the river bank I would change into a new set of clothing in the traditional style. I would cross the St. Francis dressed as the daughter of Pequawket chiefs. My best cap was colorful and carefully worked in red and blue quill and bead-work. Everyone admired it, and I always wore it proudly, so no need to replace that. Sabattis agreed to help me hunt for animals whose hides would be worked into fine buckskin. I suggested we could hunt and cure the skins during the early winter. Then I could pre-pare my new clothing during the remaining winter months. Early in the spring we could travel north by canoe, bringing any pelts or skins we had to trade at Odanak.

"The first step was to hunt for handsome deer with no flaws. I fig-ured that four large bucks would be enough. One each for the leg-gings and moccasins, one for the skirt and one for the tunic. As a warmer garment I would wear the white fur mantle Piol had given me so many years ago. This I had packed away like a treasure and seldom wore, so it remained handsome and in good repair.

"I knew all the best places for game in the Bethel area, but began by traveling around the forest and along the water's edges. I studied

tracks and followed them through the woods. I noted the bark nibbled from tree trunks and the leaves chewed off branches of lower
bushes and saplings. I looked for droppings. Soon I had a good
idea of deer routes and habits at this time of year. I set up a camp
within range of what would be my hunting ground.

"I returned to town to gather the tools and materials I would need,
and also to meet Sabattis so he could help me with my plans. We
packed sleds with poles I had cut and notched to make stretching
racks, many yards of leather strapping, axes, a sharp blade and
scraping and cutting tools. The Swans agreed to keep an eye on the
children in exchange for some of the venison we would bring back.

"We each packed a carbine and ammunition. I expected a successful trip. When we had killed and dressed the deer, we would return
to town and I would turn to the indoor job of sewing and decorat-
ing each item with colorful designs of flowers and trees. We also carried wigwam skins and dried food so we would not have to waste
time foraging. We could easily set up a lean-to at our camp site.

"The hunting ground I had selected was about ten miles out of
town, so we spent most of the first day reaching the campsite and
setting up camp. The next morning we woke to find that a few
inches of fluffy snow had fallen. God was smiling on our trip. We
would have fresh tracks. We ate a quick meal, including several
handfuls of dried grapes to give us energy for our hunt. Although we
worked together companionably, we did so in silence. Occasionally,
Sabattis would clear his throat, pause, and, with no emotion, comment humorously on whatever was on his mind. I enjoyed his jokes
all the more because I knew that he always tried to amuse me during hard times. It was his way of showing affection. I thought,
'Maybe this is a good new start.'"

Sarah's brow at first wrinkled with concern, smoothed a little.
Maybe the story would have a happy ending, after all. Oblivious to
Sarah's hope, Mollyockett continued.

"We had stacked our guns against the tent pole and loaded shells
into small sacks. We each gathered up our arms and ammunition

and set out on an ever widening spiral course, hoping to cross signs of our prey. The first hour we had no luck. Then we saw the clear hoof prints of a large moose. Sabattis cleared his throat. 'It looks,' he said, 'like the Great Spirit has his own plans for your new wardrobe. Does moose hide go well with deer hide, Molly? Should we pursue this fellow or seek smaller game?' I chuckled, 'Sabattis, I have often studied the ladies' fashion book at the general store, and moose hide will suit me very well. If we land this large animal, I will not need so many hides. Let us see what we can do.'

"We followed the moose tracks and soon found a very large bull moose grazing on purple blackberry twigs sticking up through the snow. A thicket of birch saplings lay behind him. The wind blew in our faces, so he did not smell us as we approached him slowly. I moved to the left to cover a wide angle. We had agreed that Sabattis would take the first shot. Then, if he did not succeed, I would try shooting from the other side. From behind a stand of alders, Sabattis raised his rifle and took aim. He killed the mighty animal with one shot. The moose fell with a great moan, and we saw blood on the snow. He died at once. We left him where he lay because we had noticed deer droppings as we entered the clearing. The snow had covered most of the food supply and deer congregated where they could find enough to eat.

"Sabattis returned to camp for the sled and said he would skin and butcher the moose, freeing me to go on with the hunt. In the afternoon I shot a large buck and a smaller doe. Sabattis had towed the moose hide and meat back to the campsite on the sled. He packed the meat into a basket with snow. He had stripped the flesh from the hide and removed the hair with wood ashes and water by the time I returned to report my kill.

"We returned with the sled to the place I had left the two deer. Each of us butchered one animal, again packing what we needed onto the sled and towing it back to the campsite. The large carcasses made a heavy load, but we were pleased. The Swans would welcome our gift of fresh meat. Before we returned to camp, we buried the unused portions of the moose and the deer under a cairn of branches and snow. If the ground had not been frozen, we would have buried them in the earth as a sign of respect for the spirits of the animals that provided us with food and clothing."

Sarah thought this practice was somehow more proper than the customs of her people. Her father and uncles just dumped the bones and scraps in the woods or threw them down the privy. She decided the Abenaki way was better, and no more trouble. If animals did have spirits, they would certainly be pleased that their remains were treated with dignity.

Mollyockett continued her story. "After returning to our campsite, we scraped and removed the hair from the deer skins by the light of our fire. Since all the hides were wet, I lashed them at once to the racks I had brought along. I figured up the useable area of the three hides and decided they would be more than enough for my tunic, leggings, skirt and probably two pairs of moccasins. We rose early the next morning and towed our kill back to the Swan's. As I expected, they were very pleased with the large amounts of venison and moose meat, especially the tongue, which is always a delicacy. James Swan began smoking some of the meat before the sun set. I set up the stretching racks in the shed attached to the Swan homestead.

"The next few days were warm, so I continued scraping the hides and treated them with a paste made of the pulverized brains and water. I soaked the treated hides in water for a day and then retied them to the stretching racks. While they were on the racks, I continually worked over the hides with a wooden paddle to soften them to a wonderful smooth, flexible texture. Finally, when they were fully dry and well worked, I hung the skins on racks over a smoky fire to cure the brain paste. This curing added color and made the hides waterproof. As they dried, they turned a beautiful honey color. Before long I was cutting and sewing my new clothing. I was happy for a time, but unfortunately, as soon as we settled back down to life in town, Sabattis resumed his drinking and surly behavior."

Sarah listened wide-eyed. She had heard grown-ups whisper about men who "hit the bottle" and neglected their work and their families. A few suffered terrible accidents while drinking. Mr. Griffiths fell off his horse while foolishly trying to cross the river during the spring freshet after too much drink. They found his body two days later impaled on a tree branch that, like him, had been swept downstream. The minister sometimes preached on the perils of succumbing to "Demon Rum." Sarah had never observed Uncle Thomas anything but sober and sensible. But she had overheard Aunt Sophia chastise Uncle Thomas when he drank more than one glass of the potato liquor he made in his distillery behind the house. He claimed he was checking the quality so his customers would be satisfied, but Aunt Sophia said he was "drinking up the prophets." Sarah wasn't sure exactly what "drinking up the prophets" meant, but there was a lot having to do with the Bible, especially the Old Testament, that she did not understand.

Sarah wondered how a fine man like Sabattis could become a drunkard. Could that possibly happen to James? She would have to be alert for warning signs. She took Mollyockett's hand. "How disappointed you must have been. So you finally gave up and left Sabattis?"

"No," Mollyockett replied slowly. "I probably should have, but I still loved him. When the spring came, he made excuses for not joining me on the trip north. He told me he had been hired to lead a party of settlers to scout for a location for a new mill. He said he had given his word and they would pay well. He said I should go without him. My new outfit was ready and I was pleased, especially with the colorful trims on the leggings and on the breast and cuffs of my tunic. He said I should not tarry but should join a small group that was heading north in late spring. I decided that time apart might do us good. I did not know that he had another reason for not wishing to return to Canada.

"The trip north, mainly by canoe and short portages, was uneventful. Our party paid a short visit to Metallak and his wife, Oozaluk, who had a campsite on Lake Umbagog, but otherwise we proceed-ed directly to Odanak. As I had planned, I changed into my new clothing before crossing the St. Francis River and made a fine entrance to the village. Many heads turned as I walked proudly through the village in my new clothes. I traded my pelts at the trad-ing post, and received forty silver coins in payment. Then I paid a visit to Father Charles Germaine in his study next to the church.

"Father Germaine was a crafty old Jesuit and very eager to gather funds for his mission. I told him of my desire to redeem Piol's soul from Purgatory. He said, 'You are a wise and compassionate woman and a faithful Christian. I know you cared for your late husband. You cannot imagine the torments he has been suffering while he awaits your action in his behalf. Dear child of God,' he crooned. 'How much have you earned for your pelts?' Without a word I emp-tied a sack of coins on the table in front of me. The priest looked appraisingly at the number and denomination of the coins. I could see he was adding sums in his head. He nodded. 'This looks like it will just pay to release Piol's soul. Let us pray together.' He bowed his head. I bowed mine momentarily but raised my eyes to watch him carefully."

"'Heavenly Father,' he prayed, 'inasmuch as your daughter, Marie Agathe, has offered to your Holy Catholic Church a sum of money as a token of her devotion and with confidence in your mercy, answer our prayer and release the soul of your faithful servant, Pierre Joseph, from Purgatory. Take him at once to dwell with You, Our Lord Jesus Christ, and his blessed Mother Mary and all the saints in your heavenly kingdom.' He made the sign of the Cross.

" I asked, 'Is Piol now freed from Purgatory?' The priest nodded and reached across the table for the money. Before he could gather up the coins, I scraped them back into my sack, saying, 'Thank you, Father. I'm sure the great God in Heaven has no use for the money of a poor Indian woman.'

"Father Germain's face turned red as a raspberry. He slammed his fist on the table. 'You cannot take back your offering or I will take back my prayer. Your husband will return at once to his former place of torment.'

"'No, Father, that cannot be true,' I told him. 'My husband is too wily for that. When we used to traverse the woods together, if he chanced to fall into a bad place he always stuck up a stake, that he might never be caught there any more. He will not return to Purgatory for any reason.' I left the priest's place and returned in my finery to feast with friends from days gone by."

Mollyockett smiled and chuckled deep in her throat, recalling how she had tricked the greedy priest. Sarah laughed merrily, not so much because she understood the story, but more because she enjoyed Mollyockett's pleasure in telling it.

Mollyockett's good humor dwindled quickly as she continued. "I returned to Bethel, but sadly Sabattis had only become more unruly. His behavior got worse and worse. This went on for the better part of a year. Then one night, after he had been drinking, he stalked out of the wigwam, angry at me because I would not join him under the bearskin. He staggered into the night. The next morning he returned. A stocky, round-faced Indian woman followed like a dog behind him. He barely looked at me and said, 'This is Cecile, my first wife. Make us something to eat.'"

Sarah's expression altered from astonishment to shock. How could this be? How could he...? But he promised! She gasped, "Oh my goodness! What in the world did you do?"

Mollyockett continued. "I see you are amazed at this disloyalty. You can imagine how I felt. Now I knew why he did not wish to return with me back to Odanak. Many thoughts rushed through my mind, but I did not say a word. I rose, put on my tunic, dressed the children, took my medicine bag, some bread and dried fruit and left. Later that day I found out from others who had live in the northland for a time that this Cecile was indeed Sabattis' lawful wife. They said they thought I knew.

"I learned that he had met her when trading in the Missisquoi settlement not far from Odanak and had married her in a church in Quebec years before. He often traveled so she was not surprised to have him gone for long periods of time. But when he disappeared for years she determined to find him and get him back. She traveled from Canada with a group of Abenakis and camped with them by the river in Newry, near Bethel. Sabattis had woven his way to this encampment the night before and probably enjoyed a passionate reunion while in his drunken state. The next morning he told her about me. Still groggy with drink, he brought her to our home.

"It seems that after I left, the wrongness of his behavior began to sink in. With a pounding head, Sabattis told Cecile that he had children by me and had made promises. He suggested that she return to Canada and he would see that she was provided for. She refused, reminding him that she, too, had carried his child. The young man, Baseel, who had sometimes stayed with us was her son! She said she had not come all this way for nothing and that she intended to have him. She declared, 'I will fight for you, if necessary.' This gave Sabattis an idea. Knowing that I was strong and fit, he proclaimed her idea a fine one. We would fight for him and the winner would earn him as her husband. In his foggy liquor soaked brain this seemed like a sensible solution."

Sarah could not imagine this gentle, dignified woman brawling with anyone, much less a fat alcoholic. "What a crazy notion," she blurted out. "What could he have been thinking?"

Mollyockett thought a moment then replied, "Some men have a puffed up sense of their worth. I had not thought Sabattis to be one of these, but I was wrong. I knew nothing of this plan till later in the day. I and the children joined the Swans for a morning meal, saying nothing of recent events. I asked Mrs. Swan if the children could stay with her to help stack firewood. She cheerfully agreed, since she liked the children and always welcomed them. Later in the morning as I passed by the parade ground I saw Sabattis with the woman sitting on a log, as if awaiting me."

"Sabattis rose and approached me. 'Mollyockett.' He spoke softly in his most persuasive manner. 'I know this is a surprise. I meant to tell you, but I put it off, fearing you would leave me. And now we have a problem.' I fought the urge to spit out, 'You have a problem, you skunk in a man's shape!' But I stood straight and tall and said nothing. He added in a louder voice, 'Cecile has a fine idea. She has agreed to fight with you. Whoever wins the fight will be my wife. How about it?' Then he lowered his voice again. 'You are strong and resourceful and have the best chance of winning. Then Cecile will return to Canada.'

"Meanwhile Cecile had risen from the log and approached me menacingly. She grabbed me by both arms as Sabattis stepped back. She shoved me violently. Taken by surprise I stumbled backward, then regained my footing. I looked at my would-be opponent. She was thick in the waist and had full sagging breasts. She had planted her sturdy legs wide apart and flexed her burly arms in a threatening manner. Her blood-shot eyes were set deep above plump, pock marked cheeks. Her hair, uncombed and unbound since the last evening's revels hung lank and stringy over her shoulders. My mind raced but I could not gather my thoughts. My blood pumped though my body and my palms grew moist. I began to breathe rapidly.

"Then my reason took hold and I knew what to do. As Cecile backed up to prepare for a new assault, I pulled my body up straight and tall. Feet together, shoulders square, chin slightly raised, I crossed my arms across my chest, and met her gaze with a new found confidence. In a deep, steady voice I said, 'Cecile, I am the daughter of chiefs. I will not fight for such a dishonorable man. You are welcome to him. I wish you luck. From now on I will be mother and father to my children. I will make my own way and build a life with people I can trust.' I turned and walked away without looking back. I could hear Sabattis take in a breath as if to speak. I turned and gave him a scornful look. He saw that it was over and that I would never relent. I left him with his wife. She later returned to Canada alone."

Sarah was silent. She felt angry at Sabattis and proud of Molly-ockett. Besides surviving many physical dangers and personal losses, Mollyockett had maintained her dignity, made a difficult break with one she loved, and had gone on to earn great respect among neighbors. An unmarried woman with children usually struggled for bare survival. This woman had stepped proudly along the difficult path life laid before her, creating her own detours when necessary. Now lying weak and almost helpless in the wigwam as she approached her final destination, she remained composed and ready for whatever might come.

A tear slid down Sarah's cheek. Mollyockett did not see this, but sensed Sarah's sadness. "You need not feel sorry for me, Sarah," she said. "Leaving Sabattis was difficult. But life is a gift that we must treasure in spite of setbacks. I still had many adventures and happy days ahead of me." Sarah's expression brightened as she unobtrusively wiped her eyes. "Tomorrow I will tell you of a time I cursed the hard hearted and succored the innocent and good." She shakily put down the cup of cold tea, closed her eyes and drifted off to sleep.

Chapter 11

As she waited for Sarah's arrival the next day, Mollyockett wondered how she should describe what came to be called "The Last Indian Raid." She decided to just tell what she herself had experienced at the time and what she learned from Sabattis and the Swan family thereafter. She planned to omit some of the ghastly details like how Indians had cut and carried away the scalps of James Pettingill and Peter Poor. She thought she knew why Tomhegan had attacked several homesteads along the Sunday River, in Bethel, Gilead and Shelburne, New Hampshire. She would explain his reasons, not as an excuse but just so Sarah would see that events are not always what they seem.

The morning mist rose and the sun began to dissipate the hazy clouds blanketing the mountain tops. Sarah carried her split ash basket to Mollyockett's wigwam. She had wrapped bread made yesterday in a napkin. She also brought a jar of wild berry preserves and some cornmeal gruel that Aunt Sophia said would be good for the old lady. Mollyockett was awake and alert as Sarah entered the cozy cedar wigwam. The sweet grass, tansy and other herbs hanging from the supporting poles emitted a dry sweet scent, but contended with another less pleasant odor. Sarah tried not to notice and set down

Mollyockett's breakfast. Sarah wore her old homespun work dress, a threadbare and very tight garment that she had really outgrown. Her aunt had decided Sarah should not be allowed to use her church dress every day until her mother made a new best dress. She felt ugly and irritated but tried not to take it out on her patient. She added sticks and a small log to the fire and waited for Mollyockett to eat. Mollyockett was too weak to hold a bowl, so, for the first time, Sarah fed her, spoonful by wooden spoonful.

Afterward, Mollyockett lay back and sighed wearily. "Well, I said I would tell you about the raid on Sudbury Canada, now called Bethel." Sarah remembered her Aunt Sophia's warning not to tire her patient. She knew that Aunt Sophia was right to be concerned, but she did want to hear what Mollyockett had to say about the raid so she could compare it with the terrifying stories she had heard since she was a small child.

"Mollyockett, are you sure you're strong enough today? Maybe you should rest." " No, I am all right," the old woman replied. "I think this story needs to be told, so I will tell it." She smoothed her fur robe and began.

"About thirty-five years ago, I was living mainly in Bethel but I traveled a lot and visited both white families and Indian encampments. Late in the summer, I camped with a group of Indians who I knew, but did not like much. One of them was Samsett, a rough fellow with a deep scar from his cheekbone to his chin. He sometimes traveled with Tomhegan, who considered himself chief over all the Lake Umbagog and Androscoggin region. Tomhegan was not at all my friend. He, unlike Sabattis and many other Indians, had sided with the British in the Revolution. The new Americans, proud of their successful battle for independence, called Tomhegan a Tory Indian. He, like me, believed that his land had been stolen by the white men. But unlike me he was a violent man, subject to rages. His face was always dark with anger, even without the sooty paint he added when on a rampage. Rather than trying to get along with the settlers in the region, he decided in his heart to oppose them and cause them harm. Even several years after the Americans had defeated the British and restricted them to the Northern territory in Canada, he often met with the British soldiers there and tried to use their resentment of the victorious Americans to his advantage.

"One day, Samsett had made favorable trades for his pelts. To celebrate, he brought a large flask of rum into the camp. He did give me and the others a small drink, but in a short time swallowed down the rest himself. Soon he was singing and boasting. While in this state he declared that his friend, Tomhegan, was going to revenge himself on the Americans and at the same time earn a large bounty by capturing settlers and carrying them to the British in Canada as his forefathers had carried early settlers to the French. Samsett gave a wild whoop. I pretended to be unconcerned and said, 'This sounds like a bold, clever plan. Tell me about it.' He raised his fist and said, 'I do not know his full plan, but Tomhegan says he will get even with that Boston dandy, Colonel Clark.'

"Now Sarah, Colonel Clark was my friend and a friend to many Indians because of his fair dealing and good nature." Sarah wondered aloud, "Well then, why was Tomhegan so angry with him?" Mollyockett replied, "Colonel Clark had recently scolded Tomhegan in front of others for stealing from a cache of supplies the Colonel had left in reserve at the end of the last hunting season. Tomhegan was proud and did not like to be chastised even when in the wrong. Humiliation turned into hatred. Samsett said, 'Before the moon sets, while the falling stars signal death, Tomhegan will swoop like a hawk from his camp and kill Colonel Clark and his companions in their nest in the mountains! Then he will do worse.' He whooped again then suddenly collapsed, totally overcome by the rum." Sarah was shocked, but tried to maintain her composure.

Mollyockett continued, "Samsett's companions paid no attention as I sat for a while, then quietly left the fire as if to find a sleeping place. On his way north, Colonel Clark had told me that he intended to set up a hunting camp near the peak we called Agiochook, place of the Great Spirit. It has since been named Mt.

Washington in honor of the great general and new president. With only a small pack of food, a sleeping robe and my rifle, I set out to warn my friend of his danger. It was almost five hours journey, even if I traveled swiftly, so I took the shortest trail, although it was a rougher path, sometimes over rugged ground and through dense forests. As the darkness deepened I wondered whether I would reach him in time as I often had to retrace my steps and find the trail. Then the moon rose and I could see better, so I moved as quickly as my legs would carry me, often at a loping gait that provides speed without tiring.

"As I drew near the place I knew Colonel Clark's camp to be, I slowed my pace, watching for movement that might be Tomhegan and his party. Despite the hour, Colonel Clark was busy bundling pelts by the light of the fire and the moon. He planned to get an early start in the morning. After reuniting with his companions, they would pool their trade goods and return to Boston. I made a bird sound. He turned and peered into the trees momentarily alarmed. When he saw it was a friend, he smiled and started to welcome me to his fire. He had always treated me with courtesy and respect. His tall, lean body unfolded from his task and he rose to greet me. Without a moment's delay I warned him of Tomhegan's plan. He responded at once, tightening his boot laces and reaching for his rifle. He did not pause to break up camp, but grabbed one large bundle of furs and followed me into the thicket that grew along a stream. He said his companions were camped about two miles distant and I agreed that we should attempt to warn them as well.

"He wanted to take the path along the stream to his companion's campsite, but I feared that if the murderers had reached the other camp first, they would follow the stream as the shortest route to the Colonel's camp. He saw the wisdom of my suggestion. We took a less traveled route through the forest as the moon began to move lower toward the horizon. Two stars shot across the sky. When we arrived at the camp, we were too late. Both men had been brutally killed, their bodies lying face down on the blood-soaked ground not far from the campfire. Since Tomhegan's party had the advantage of numbers and darkness and since there was no one nearby, they had used their hatchets instead of their rifles."

"With great sadness Colonel Clark pulled the bodies of his companions nearer the fire, hoping to ward off animals and covered them with a blanket, saying a prayer as he did so. His usually ruddy cheeks were ashen and his jaw was tight as he struggled to hold back his grief. The fire had dwindled to a few embers. The sounds of the forest seemed to swell and diminish. We both stood silently for a moment. Then, at my urging, we retreated quickly and silently into the woods as the moon disappeared behind a ridge of pines.

"Colonel Clark and I spent the rest of the night at an abandoned shelter. We slept badly although we were tired from our efforts. We had used our blankets to cover the dead, so we were cold and hungry. Also we kept straining to hear sounds that might warn us of Tomhegan's approach. Soon after tending to the burial of his friends, Colonel Clark returned to Boston.

"We never saw Tomhegan that night. He seemed to vanish in the woods, but weeks later he emerged and attacked Gilead, Shelburne and Sudbury Canada. He killed two men, stole guns and items of value from settlers' homes and carried off prisoners to Canada, including Nathaniel Segar, Colonel Clark's cousin, Benjamin, and a colored man named Plato, who worked for Peter Poor. Although Tomhegan's party frightened the families in the homesteads they raided, they did not harm women or children and even released a boy they intended to take when his father begged for his life. I believe that Tomhegan chose the Benjamin Clark homestead as a target because it stood on land that had once been a sacred burying ground for Indians.

"When the settlers in Sudbury Canada learned of Tomhegan's raid, they sent to Fryeburg and formed a rescue party made up of men from the two settlements. Sabattis led the party and he later told me how he hunted for signs of the trail of the captives then lost and found it again. As the rescue party struggled to find the trail, Benjamin Clark staggered out of the woods, very much worn and haggard. He said the Indians had released him so he could deliver a message not to follow or the captives would be killed. The rescuers discussed turning back, but their blood was up. They would not be deterred, and continued until they found a message written by Mr. Segar. Tomhegan had forced Mr. Segar to scratch a warning on spruce bark and nailed it to a tree. The warning said that if the party were overtaken by Americans, the Indians would kill their prisoners. Again, Sabattis told me, the members of the rescue party discussed among themselves what to do. They took a vote and decided to turn back to bury the dead and to fortify the settlements against further attacks.

"Ever after these attacks, when he returned to the area, the Colonel sought me out and attempted to show his thanks with coins, with furs, with a new rifle and other gifts. All these I refused, saying, 'Friends help friends for the sake of friendship alone. Your continued good company is my reward.' When he saw that I would not accept his gifts, he made a solemn promise to come to my aid if ever I should need help. I was pleased by the promise, but I was still healthy and strong and did not believe I would ever have cause to rely on it."

Sarah thought about Mollyockett's refusal to accept gifts from Colonel Clark. She herself loved gifts and could not imagine refusing one unless it was tainted in some way. She thought, "Maybe Mollyockett liked having others in her debt. Jesus says that it is more blessed to give than to receive." She remembered her Aunt Sophia telling how Mollyockett sometimes would accept no payment for her medicines. "Mollyockett," Sarah asked, "did Colonel Clark ever manage to repay his debt to you?"

"Well," replied the old woman, "he certainly tried. Not too many years ago he came up from Massachusetts to trade. He visited me as usual, but I could see he was surprised that I was beginning to show my age. I still felt well, but my movements were slower and my face was becoming lined. I even had gray hairs.

"He said, 'Mollyockett, you have traveled to Connecticut, to Vermont, to Canada and all over Maine. Why not come down to Boston with me when I return. You can stay in my home in the city. I promise I will keep your bones warm and your belly well fed.' I remembered my girlhood visit to Boston on the 'Golden Swallow.' When I told him of my earlier trips to the city, he was at first surprised to learn that I had already been there. Then he said, 'Well, my friend, I do not know why anything about you should surprise me. You have always been a remarkable woman! Come live in my house!' I admit I was flattered. Partly to get him to stop pestering me, and partly because I enjoyed his company, I agreed to go with him when he returned to Boston in November.

"The Colonel was true to his word and treated me like a princess. There was no shortage of fine food and rum or wine every night. I thought, 'I could get used to this! Why do I need to find my own food and light my own fire?' Colonel Clark and I enjoyed each other's company. We loved to share our recollections of hunting trips and people we had known. He often asked me to tell stories of long ago. He especially liked tales of great battles, no matter who won or lost. The stories I told had been handed down from my ancestors, but I liked to tell them as if I had seen them with my own eyes. His favorite was a tale I called 'The Battle at the Pond.'" Mollyockett paused.

Sarah waited. She thought maybe Mollyockett had drifted off, but her eyes were open. Sarah said, "Will you tell that story to me?"

Mollyockett settled herself and took a breath. "Well now, let's see what I can remember. Ah, yes. Now I've got it. Some years ago when settlements were few in this land, Captain John Lovewell, a well respected soldier, marched from Dunstable, a town in Massachusetts. He hoped to bring the land of the Pequawkets, then a mighty tribe, under his control. He started out with a troop of forty-three men, but illness and injury took their toll. By the time he got to a fort set up at Ossipee, his war party was reduced to thirty-four men from various Massachusetts towns.

"They left the safety of the fort and headed into the land of the Pequawkets. For several days, they heard the Pequawkets all around them in the forest, but they did not see a soul until early on a Saturday. As they prayed together on the eve of the Sabbath, they heard a gunshot. They saw a lone Indian standing on a point on the banks of Saco Pond. They argued about what to do. Were they being drawn into a trap? Should they return to the fort, or should they move ahead. Afraid of being called cowards by their neighbors at home, they set down their packs and moved forward. They thought the Pequawkets, led by the great chief Paugus, lay ahead. I should remind you, Sarah, that this brave fighter, Paugus, was my grandfather.

"Sure enough, before long an Indian warrior came toward them. They squatted, shouldered their weapons and shot at him. The volley brought the Pequawket warrior down, but not before he had discharged several rounds of beaver shot, wounding Captain Lovewell as well as Mr. Samuel Whiting. Some say these wounds later proved fatal to Captain Lovewell. Anyway, Mr. Frye of Andover, the company chaplain, went forward to where the dead Indian lay and scalped him. I have often wondered if the chaplain felt that scalping was part of his duty as God's agent. Feeling confident, the troop marched proudly with their scalp to the place they had left their packs, unaware that the Pequawket party had already found the gear at the edge of a clearing.

"Paugus had divided his warriors into two parties. One charged Lovewell's troops from the front, while the other attacked from the rear. They killed several white soldiers. Captain Lovewell was among the fallen. The English left their dead and retreated to the Pond. The fighting continued with much hubbub, the Pequawkets giving whoops and howling like wolves, the English shouting and calling 'Huzzah! Huzzah!'

"Paugus had led several raids on Dunstable and other Massachusetts towns in retribution for English attacks, so he was well known by many of these men. Though an enemy, he was respected as a brave warrior. During pauses in the fighting, the men who had fought Paugus in earlier battles exchanged jibes and comments with the chief. As Paugus and James Chamberlain faced each other, the weapons of both became fouled with too much firing. Each man, still boasting of his intent to kill the other, went to the water's edge and washed their weapons. When the weapons were clean, they again took up opposing positions, loaded and fired. My grandfather fell, never again to rise in this world. Chamberlain was amazed that he had killed the man known as the undaunted sachem of his enemy.

"At sunset, the Pequawkets took stock. Their chief was fallen, but they had killed twelve English and wounded many others. Counting this a victory, they disappeared into the forest. The English, relieved that they were alone, gathered the wounded who could not travel and left them in safe places, hoping that a rescue party from the fort would find them. Those who could walk struggled back to the fort. Much to their surprise they found the fort deserted. It seems that one of Lovewell's party had retreated at the height of the battle and returned to the fort. He gave such a gruesome account of the battle, that all departed at once for their homes in Massachusetts. This battle was reported as a great victory for the English.

"Colonel Clark said he had heard the English version of this story many times. Settlers recited poems and sang songs describing the battle. They made the English heroes and the Indians devils. Brave devils, but devils nonetheless. He said my story showed bravery and weakness on both sides and was probably closer to the truth.

"So I sat by his fireplace and we traded stories for many evenings. During the day I went about the town to see the sights. Boston had grown and developed since my girlhood visit. Many fine houses lined the cobbled streets. Some were brick, or clapboard, but a few had splendid marble facades. I marveled at the cleverness of the builders. I often visited the busy market place at Fanuil Hall. The giant hall housed many merchants. Still others set up stalls in the neighborhood. Every manner of goods was offered for sale: meat, eggs, vegetables, herbs, spices, teas, baskets, skeins of yarn and yards of woven linen and wool, tools, tinware, leather goods and much more. A large part of this bounty came in from the countryside by cart, but more had been carried from all over the world by the huge trading ships that still lined the harbor.

"Nevertheless, as time went by, I began more and more to long for the forests and lakes of the Dawnland. I believed, and still believe, that my ancestors called me home. Seeing my growing unhappiness, Colonel Clark agreed to return me to Bethel when he traveled back in the spring. He did make me promise that I would allow him to build me a snug shelter and said, like it or not, he was my protector. He said he would always care for me as his beloved aunt. I liked the idea of having such a nephew and accepted his kindness." Sarah smiled. "He sounds like a wonderful man. Did he honor his promise?"

Mollyockett nodded, "He did. He built me a fine wigwam near Rumford Falls and visited me many times. He brought gifts of meat, rum and sometimes dainties I had grown fond of in Boston. I always remarked that Colonel Clark's loyalty shows how even an evil deed can beget unimagined goodness."

"What happened to the captives, and to Tomhegan?" Sarah asked.

"Well," Mollyockett recalled, "After a period as prisoners of the British in Canada, Mr. Segar and the others were returned as part of a prisoner exchange, although I believe that poor Plato was sold as a slave to a Canadian. For some reason, white men treated blacks even worse than they treated Indians. Mr. Segar later wrote of his adventures, hoping the government would make him some payment for his military service and the time he spent in captivity. I doubt he got a cent."

"And Tomhegan?" Sarah asked.

Mollyockett folded her arms across her chest as she usually did when she faced a difficult situation. "After some time went by, angry settlers finally tracked Tomhegan down. They found several scalps in his bag, so they knew he had continued his bloody attacks. For these actions and for his earlier violence he died a death I would wish on no man. A group of vengeful settlers tied him on a horse in such a manner that his spurs continually goaded the poor animal. They smacked the horse with a stick and he took off at a frenzied pace into an orchard. The low hanging branches tore Tomhegan to pieces."

Sarah shuddered involuntarily. "Oh, my! How horrible. That doesn't sound like the noble idea of justice that our teacher tells us the Revolution was fought to bring about."

"No, child. Violence and torture never bring credit on a people, neither yours nor mine. Retribution belongs to God, who is our final judge."

Sarah nodded in agreement but her eyes were wide. Saving lives using medicine is good work. Risking your life for another is God's work. "Mollyockett, you were so brave. And you deserved a friend for life. Did the Colonel remain your protector forever as he promised?" Sarah awaited an answer. She glanced at Mollyockett whose eyes had closed. She was asleep again.

Chapter 12

Mollyockett was drowsy, but awake the next morning when Sarah brought her breakfast. Outside the wigwam, a large crow cawed raucously. The sound echoed among the pines, still dripping from a light rain the night before. Sarah was surprised a crow would be so near the Bragg's busy household. Perhaps an animal had left its kill not fully eaten.

As Sarah drew near her resting place, Mollyockett noticed that the girl was wearing a different dress, covered by the same linen apron she wore everyday. Sarah seemed to have grown overnight from a girl to a young woman. "My, Sarah, I don't see clearly, but it seems to me that you look even prettier than usual today. Is that a new dress?" Sarah was pleased that Mollyockett had noticed. The old woman still took an interest in the world around her, a good sign.

"Yes, Mollyockett, it is a different dress. My mother has begun sewing me a new best dress made of linsey woolsy with little sprigs of flowers printed on it. Mr. Abbott at the store had a web of cloth from Boston and Grandmother used her egg and butter credit to trade for some, so both Mother and I will have new dresses for the winter. Mother said I could start wearing my best dress for everyday. Aunt Sophia says she will cut my old dress down for my little cousin

Sophia, poor thing. None of us like hand-me-downs, but 'Waste not, want not' as Uncle Thomas says. There's not much wear left in that old dress, though I tried to keep it clean and well mended. Sophia is too little to care, but an older girl would wish I had worn it to tatters so she could have something new."

"Well," said Mollyockett, "This dress is very becoming and I'm sure your new dress will be prettier still. Will you wear a kerchief with it?"

Sarah thought a moment, "I think Mother is dyeing a piece of lawn indigo blue. Then I'll probably tat an edging in white."

Mollyockett nodded approvingly. "Will you wear beads? I always thought the Methodist ladies looked so pretty wearing a string of beads on a Sunday."

"Oh," said Sarah. "I love beads, too, but I don't have any. Mother says some day I will have hers."

Still nodding, Mollyockett smiled cryptically. "Well then, go find the small sack toward the bottom of the ash basket with the blue and red design on the top."

Sarah hesitantly approached the assortment of baskets near Mollyockett's feet. She knew that Mollyockett stored all kinds of belongings in these baskets and she didn't want to seem to be rummaging through her personal things. She found a medium sized basket covered with a geometric design of blue crosses with red dots in each of the four quadrants. It was a simple, but pleasing pattern. She held the basket up by the handle. "Is this the one you wanted?"

Mollyockett squinted, trying to bring the basket into focus. "Yes, child, just open the lid and find the small sack. It's made of moose hide, if I recall, with a drawstring of darker leather thongs." Sarah pulled out a little bag and held it up. Mollyockett squinted. "Yes, that's it. Loosen the string and bring it here." Sarah replaced the basket and curiously loosened the drawstring. She opened the bag and handed it to Mollyockett who straightened herself slightly and partially emptied the contents into one hand.

Involuntarily, Sarah moved closer. Mollyockett's dark, wrinkled hand contained a small pile of lustrous spheres, each pierced with a small hole. She held out her hand toward Sarah. "Here, take these to make a necklace to wear with your new dress. Sarah took the loose beads into her own hand. Meanwhile Mollyockett pushed the bag containing the remaining beads toward Sarah, and continued, "I made these beads from shells I gathered some years ago when I was camping near the sea. There should be enough."

Sarah gazed down at the iridescent beads softly glowing pale pink, paler blue and milky white even in the dim light. "Oh, Mollyockett! They're beautiful! They look like pearls! You made them?" Her delight faded quickly. "Golly, they're so pretty and it must have taken hours to carve and polish them. I'm not sure my folks will let me keep them."

"Don't worry, Sarah. I'll talk to your aunt when she visits this afternoon. Your family will allow me to make you this small gift." Mollyockett's warm smile showed her pleasure that her offering was well received. "Put them back into the sack for safe-keeping and take them with you when you go. Now, let's settle down to business. I was going to tell you about the time I met unkindness on one day and kindness on the next and how I punished one and rewarded the other."

Still clutching the beads in one hand and the sack in the other, Sarah sat on the ground next to Mollyockett. Sarah returned the loose beads to the sack. Holding the precious gift in both of her hands, she focused her full attention on Mollyockett as she began another tale.

"About five or six years ago, after most of the leaves had fallen, but the oak leaves were still rattling on the branches, I decided to journey south from Andover to visit Dr. Hamlin who lives on Paris Hill. I had often traveled to Paris and to nearby Poland, but had never stopped at the Hamlin place, since it was a bit off the trail. I had heard of Dr. Hamlin through Mr. Henry Tufts who had spent some time with me trying to learn my medical practices.

"A while back, Mr. Tufts had suffered a serious knife wound which had festered. He was often delirious with pain. He tried to treat himself with no luck. Hearing that I had good medicine he asked for my help. Even though some have said Mr. Tufts was not always an honorable man, I pitied his suffering and agreed to help him by preparing daily doses of medicine. He complained mightily about the bitterness of my tonic and the sting of my poultices, but said he would try anything to recover.

"Each day I visited him, and each day he complained, but swallowed the medicine I had prepared. Before long he said he was mending and no longer suffered with pains and fever. His digestion improved and he gathered strength. The fever disappeared. After a month, the pains went away, the wound healed and he once again had the appetite of a horse. Still I urged him to continue the medicine for a while longer. He did so until we both agreed that he was cured.

"After that, Mr. Tufts spent many hours with me, hoping, I think, that I would teach him my cures. Although I tried to be polite, I seldom revealed much of any importance. As you already know, I had generally been unwilling to tell others how I prepared my medicines. I feared that they would laugh or that they would use my medicines wrongly to cause harm and I would be blamed. Also I considered my secrets an inheritance from my mother. The settlers may have taken my land, but they would not take my medicine.

"Once, while I was in Vermont visiting my daughter, an epidemic of a disease that drained the fluids from the body swept through the settlement of Troy. It was especially deadly for children. Remembering how I had failed to save my granddaughter, I resolved to do my best to help these children. I treated and healed many. The settlers begged me for the recipe for my medicine. I refused. But the next year I was traveling through the same area. I was slowed down by bad weather and ran short of food. I tried to ration the little that remained but I was weak with hunger. I stumbled along until I met a settler about a day's trip from the village. He was scouting for game and was well supplied. He carried a large slab of pork, as well as meal and biscuits. Seeing my poor state, he immediately shared his supplies. He cut off a thick slab of pork. I ate a portion of the meat at once. The pork was delicious and renewed my strength. I gave him several packets of herbs and promised that his kindness would be further rewarded. The next day I reached Troy. I asked several women of the village to meet with me. I told them of their neighbor's generosity. In gratitude for his kindness, I offered to share my dysentery cure, a decotation of the inner bark of the spruce tree. From that time forward, they were able to treat their own families. Now I have shared my secret with you, too, Sarah."

Sarah wondered how the bark was prepared. It didn't sound very promising medicine to her, but she kept her reservations to herself.

"Despite my unwillingness to share my medicines, Mr. Tufts told many acquaintances of his good 'doctoress,' as he called me. Those he told included Dr. Hamlin. He urged me to meet with Dr. Hamlin to discuss my medical practices. Perhaps he thought I would share with a doctor what I would not share with him. I had put off meeting with Dr. Hamlin for several years but many people told me he was a good and wise man. Finally, I decided that I was not getting any younger and should make this trip.

"I packed a few belongings, some food and herbs in a back-basket. Since I felt a slight ache in my bones, I suspected that the weather might turn cold, so I wore long deerskin leggings under my woolen dress, a warm fur cape, double soled moccasins and my embroidered cap. I folded the side flaps of the cap up to form peaks on each side of my head, but I knew I could always pull them down over my ears if a chill did develop. My friend, Mrs. Merrill, had knit a warm pair of fleece lined mittens for me and I tossed them in my pack, just in case. I traveled easily from Andover to Bethel and spent the night there with the Chapmans.

"After a hasty breakfast with the Chapman family, I set out early. The sun was just melting the frost that coated the ground. My path sparkled with tiny rainbows. I felt happy with the sun warming my back and walked at a lively pace, though I did not run like a deer as I did in younger days. My destination was a long

long day's journey but I had often traveled further with no trouble. I glanced over my shoulders and noticed at the crest of a hill that the peaks of the distant White Mountains behind me were frosted with the first snow. This did not concern me, because the mountains always have snow far before the lower lands along the river valley and beside the ponds.

"The Bethel village was soon behind me and my route was largely uninhabited except for an occasional farmhouse. Before noon I had passed through the village called Woodstock. The settlers in this part of the country used a very old Indian trail as a main route between the farmsteads and small villages that were growing up in the foothills of the mountains and along the Ellis, Androscoggin and Little Androscoggin Rivers. Many years ago, my grandfather, the great chief Paugus, had traveled this route and gathered his warriors on the cliffs overlooking the pond that feeds the Little Androscoggin. From there, he led them to Lovewell's Pond where he fought nobly in a great battle and was killed. Even his enemies praised his bravery, and his deeds are still told in stories and poems. I have always been proud to walk in his footsteps."

"Oh dear," Sarah thought. "She's forgotten that she told me about Paugus and Captain Lovewell. It's not like her to forget. I hope she's not getting all confused like some old people." Oblivious of her mental lapse, Mollyockett continued.

"When I first traveled this way as a young woman, it was no more than a narrow footpath along the gravel bank of the river. In those days I had a favorite campsite on the crest of a small mountain two hours' walk on a side trail to the east of the main trail. In the years since then, that narrow side trail had become a road leading to the homes of the Cushman and Perham families. Likewise, the main trail had changed. Carts and horses as well as those on foot like myself used the main trail so frequently that it became more established each year. The road I traveled to Paris was easily wide enough for a wagon, although there were few at that time. The dirt in the tracks formed by countless cart wheels was packed down, or muddy or dusty, depending on the season. On that day, the ground had frozen overnight, so the way was firm. I walked beside the track because even frozen grass and weeds is easier to walk on than bare frozen ground.

"Around midday, I chewed some jerky and ate a biscuit, but did not stop because I saw that the gray clouds had entirely covered the sky. The air felt cold and moist in a way that I knew meant that snow was likely. In early afternoon it began. First, a flurry whirled cheerfully around me, then large clumps of snow rapidly covered the ground. A cold wind blew up and the snow flew fiercely in my face so I had to squint to allow my lashes to protect my eyes.

"Usually on long walking trips, I occupy my mind by observing the wonders of the field and forest, the grassy plumes of wild wheat waving in the wind, a golden mushroom pushing through the soil, the chipmunks scampering among the roots of the trees, the fringe winged hawk wheeling overhead. The snow deprived me of such entertainment. The dense whiteness hid the view even two feet ahead. White knives of icy snow kept coming at me, coming at me. It was a storm to reckon with.

"I could hardly see, but drew my cape over my head and around my shoulders and kept moving steadily. The snow accumulated quickly and darkness fell early. By the time I reached Trap Corner in the late afternoon I was breaking a trail through eight inches of snow. I frequently slipped or stumbled. Although I was moving more slowly, I was damp with sweat. At the same time, as the wind cut through my clothes, I chilled to the bone. My breath came heavily and I grew more and more tired as the snow mounted. I decided to continue to the mill at the great falls about two miles ahead and seek shelter for the night with the miller's family.

"I was relieved to hear the thundering of the Little Androscoggin rushing over the jagged rocks and dropping twenty feet to the lower level. 'Almost there,' I said to myself, 'Keep going.' In a few minutes I could just see a light shining through the tiny window of the miller's cabin. The mill itself, set back directly over the waterfall, was invisible in the snow. I could smell wood smoke and could almost feel the warmth of the hearth.

"I staggered up to the front of the house, slipping on the stone step. I pounded on the door. I heard hushed voices within, but no one came. I called out, 'It is Mollyockett. I have traveled far in the storm and seek shelter.' Again I heard hushed voices, but no footsteps coming to the door. Again I cried out. 'I need a place to stay overnight. I am an old woman, a friend to all. I am very tired.' This time a harsh male voice said, ' Go away! Indians are not welcome here.'

"I had traveled widely for many years and had never been turned away, especially on a night like this. I could not believe what I heard. Most people knew me and welcomed me. Others read in the Bible that Jesus said to offer hospitality to people you do not know. Such good Christians will be recompensed at the resurrection of the just. This is what Indian people have always believed and we turn no one away. I tried again. 'I mean no harm, I have my own food. All I ask is a dry place to rest.' Again the voices conferred for a minute then the man shouted, 'No, go away. You can't stay here!'

"I realized that these people had set their hearts against me. Exhausted, I turned from the door and thought what I should do. I could not continue in this storm or I would surely die. They would not let me in, but they could not prevent me from staying nearby. I walked around the side of the cabin until I found the chimney. With my hands I cleared away the snow beside the warm chimney stones. I removed my backpack, shook out my cape and, curled up on the bare ground. I placed my backpack behind me to partially protect me from the whirling snow. Then I covered myself with my robe as best I could. The stones were warm but still I spent an uncomfortable night and slept little. I knew I would survive, but the more I thought about the harsh treatment I had received, the angrier I became."

"Poor Mollyockett," said Sarah. "It makes me shiver and feel furious just to think of it. How could they be so cruel?" Mollyockett shook her head with anger and dismay. After all these years she still

Snow Falls, West Paris, Maine

An early mill stood at Snow Falls, located on the Little Androscoggin River in West Paris, Maine. Mollyockett sought shelter here, was turned away and uttered her famous curse. A park containing the Falls and the site of the mill is located beside Route 26.

(Photo by the author)

resented being turned away. "I have never understood and have never forgiven them.

"Just before dawn," she continued, "the snow tapered off and first rays of the sun painted the sky with rosy streaks. The wind had died and the air felt crisp and cold on my cheeks. The snow all about was about three hands deep. I took some jerky and a biscuit from my pack and ate them along with dried wild grapes. I did not attempt to build a fire, but decided to arise immediately to continue to Paris Hill, another four or five miles. As I arose, my bones ached. I could hardly straighten my legs. My anger returned. I wrapped myself tightly in my robe and lifted my pack onto my shoulders. I walked around the cabin and started away from the door and up the slope toward the obscured roadway.

"Before I resumed my journey, I turned and faced the miller's cabin. I said aloud in a voice made harsh by my hard night, 'Oh, stone hearted people! Your unkindness toward a weary traveler will be punished. Jesus said, "If you have done this to the least of these, you have done it to me." Those who dwell on this land have offended the laws of God. From now on this place will not prosper. You will be visited with affliction and your work will not bear fruit. I turn my back on you and go on to a kinder place.'"

Sarah was stunned, not only with the hard-hearted behavior of the miller and his family, but with Mollyockett's uncharacteristic vehemence. She imagined her old friend shaking her fist and cursing those who had abused her. She imagined Mollyockett, shivering with cold, but at the same time inflamed with indignation. "What happened to the family at the falls?" she asked. "Did your curse work?"

Mollyockett looked straight ahead. "From that day to this, any enterprise at that place has turned to dust. I have sometimes wondered whether I did right. But I have not yet decided it is wrong to curse those who hate Indians or any person so much that they will let them freeze in the night. If I had not found shelter near the chimney, I would surely have died. I did not wish those who abused me dead. I just prayed that they would not prosper. I have not yet

Dr. Cyrus Hamlin's Residence

This early photo of the birthplace of Hannibal Hamlin shows a substantial dwelling. Here Mollyockett saved the dying infant's life. He grew up to serve as Governor of Maine and Abraham Lincoln's first Vice President. The main house has been refurbished and the outbuildings and grounds enhanced. Together they form an extremely elegant focal point for Paris Hill today. The house is privately owned.

(Photo provided by the Bethel Historical Society and Regional History Center)

seen cause to withdraw my curse. And no one, learning of my words, has said I was wrong. But remember, Sarah, despite this meanness and a curse, the story has a good ending."

"That's right," said Sarah. "You are here with me, so you certainly did not perish in the snow. Thank God for that."

"Thank God, indeed," said Mollyockett reverently. "He gave me strength to continue my journey, although each step in the deep snow was an act of will. I returned to the snow covered main road and continued two miles to the turnoff to the left that led to the top of Paris Hill. I trudged up the hill, hoping with all my heart, that I could keep going for the next few miles and make my way to the crest of the hill. It was steeper than I expected. Dark thoughts rattled through my brain. Suppose the Hamlin family was not at home?

Suppose they were home, but they, too, turned me away?

"I had not much strength remaining when the Hamlin's large clapboard house, surrounded with outbuildings and fences, came into view. The sun reflected off the snow and the gleaming white house, roofed with a snowy crest seemed to grow out of the hilltop. A feather of white smoke stood out against the intense crystal blue sky. It was a beautiful and welcome sight to my tired old eyes. Without thinking, I walked more rapidly, lifting one foot directly out of the hole it had left in the snow and placing it resolutely a full step ahead and then repeating these motions over and over until I found myself climbing the steps to the front door. I pounded as firmly as I could on the door and waited as the sound echoed within.

"Very soon, a young woman came to the door. I did not know who she might be, whether a member of the household, or a hired girl. Her apron was clean and she had tucked her hair into a tidy linen cap. No matter, she looked at me with pity and concern and said, 'Old woman, you look exhausted. Come in, come in to the hall and warm yourself by the fire. I will get the doctor.'

"I began to try to remove my icy moccasins so as not to track snow into the house. 'Don't bother with that,' this young angel urged. 'I can mop up later. Come right in. Let me take your cape. Here sit in this chair by the fire. I'll bring you some tea.' I walked stiffly over to the large wooden rocker and almost fell into it.

"I immediately fell asleep. When I awoke a few moments later, a gentleman I knew must be Dr. Hamlin was looking down on me with kindly interest. Behind him stood the girl with a cup of steaming tea. I took the cup gratefully and noticed with even more gratitude that someone had added a dollop of rum. My hand shook as I raised the spicy brew to my lips with both hands. I swallowed and sighed with satisfaction. Dr. Hamlin said, 'Can this be Mollyockett, the savior of that interesting rogue, Henry Tufts?' As I nodded he asked, 'Are you able to talk, or would you rather rest a while?'

"I was still shivering, but attempted a smile and a greeting. 'I have had better moments, but I am happy to find your door. A little of this fine tea,' I nodded to the girl, 'and I will be restored. I thank you for taking me in.'"

"'Dear woman,' he said, 'You are more than welcome, but sadly you come at a bad time for our family.' His handsome face darkened, and tears sprang to his eyes, ringed by black circles.

"I immediately straightened in the chair and started to rise. I sensed great sorrow. 'Please tell me of your trouble. Perhaps I can help.'

"He gestured to show that I should stay seated. He pulled over a second chair, sat and cleared his throat. 'Several months ago,' he began, 'Mrs. Hamlin was delivered of a fine son. He seemed healthy, lusty and full of life. Then suddenly he became fretful and refused to nurse. Now he lies listless and we fear we will lose him. I have tried everything, to no avail. I cannot help my own dear son.' He sighed deeply. I remembered my own despair when I could not save my daughter's baby.

"My fatigue lifted at once. I felt renewed. I knew the Holy Spirit was with me. Strength and energy swept through my body. I arose at once and handed the cup still half full of tea to the young woman. I looked deeply into Dr. Hamlin's troubled eyes. 'If you will allow me to see him, perhaps I can do something.'"

"'By all means,' the doctor replied. 'Many people have told me of your healing skills. Any idea, any assistance will be welcome.' He turned and led me down a hall lighted with a whale oil lamp even in the daytime. He paused at an oak door and knocked softly.

"A weary, soft, sad voice answered, 'Yes?' The Doctor pushed the door open saying, 'My dear, we have an unexpected, but welcome guest. It's Mollyockett, the Indian medicine woman. She has arrived like an angel of mercy at our doorstep and has offered to treat the baby. May we enter?'

"'Of course, do come in,' she replied. We entered and I saw the thin, pale mother abed with the infant wrapped in a blanket, lying beside her.

"Her tired eyes widened at the sight of a bedraggled old Indian woman. Then she politely tried to conceal her surprise. I am sure I did not match her picture of the ideal representative of the medical profession. She recovered her poise and smiled weakly. She glanced anxiously down at her tiny son. 'I fear he is going to leave us soon.' she whispered. 'I am praying for his soul.'

"I approached the bedside. The baby was pale and barely breathing. 'May I hold him?' I asked. I brushed the front of my dress to be sure no snow or moisture remained.

"She said, 'Surely. I know many people speak well of your cures. If there's anything....' Her voice trailed off as she gathered up the little bundle and held the baby toward me. I reached out and took him gently in my arms.

"It felt wonderful to hold an infant, even an ill one. 'What is his name?' I asked.

"'We have called him Hannibal,' said Dr. Hamlin, 'after the great general. I fear he is losing his first major battle.'

"'Ah, Hannibal, little Hannibal,' I cooed. 'You are light as a bird. You must eat and grow fat.' I held him close and swayed back and forth.

"His mother explained sadly, 'I do not have much milk. I have given him life, but it seems I cannot sustain it.'

"I put my finger to his lips. He pursed them and I could hear weak sucking sounds. My hopes rose. I said, 'We must act quickly. Please bring me a pitcher of cow's milk warmed slightly. Doctor, may I use one of your larger medicine bottles? And I will need a piece of clean linen and a length of cord or yarn.' Mrs. Hamlin looked up hopefully, wondering what I had in mind.

"A few moments later, when the items I has asked for were assembled on the bedside table, I returned the baby to his mother. He wailed weakly. I set to work. I poured a small amount of warm milk into the thin medicine bottle. I tore a small square from the linen cloth. I broke off a short length of yarn and tied it tightly around the center section of the cloth, to a length of the end of my little finger. Then I tied the cloth to the bottle by wrapping the cord around the neck of the bottle. I saw Mrs. Hamlin's anxiety, and decided that the child might feel her emotion and become even more fretful. I asked if I might hold the child again to treat him. Both mother and father nodded their agreement.

"I settled into a rocking chair next to the bed with the babe in my arms. Talking softly to him, I placed the linen nipple near his mouth. As the bottle tipped, the milk soaked the cloth and a drop fell on the baby's lips. His tiny pink tongue appeared and tasted the milk. As his mouth opened, I gently inserted the cloth nipple between his lips. He paused as if to say, 'What is this?' Then he began to suck.

"His mother closed her eyes, bowed her head, and said, 'Thank God. My baby is eating. My precious baby is eating.' I handed the baby, still drinking from the bottle, to Mrs. Hamlin. She smiled fondly and nested him in her arms as he continued feeding."

"Dr. Hamlin looked on amazed, but beaming. He looked at his wife, his child, and then, at me. 'Mollyockett, you amaze me. You are truly, as many have said, a great doctoress. Your reputation is fully justified. Thank you.' My heart warmed at his kind words.

"Dr. Hamlin thought for a moment. Then he said, 'You are a professional person like myself. What do I owe you for your services?' Over the years I have usually refused payment when I heal, except for one penny. These coins I have saved in a sack more as a memento than as reward. I told Dr. Hamlin that I would accept nothing but one penny. He smiled and said, 'Somehow this generosity does not surprise me. But you must accept our hospitality. After the baby has finished, I will show you to a comfortable chamber and you must rest. Doctor's orders. I will prepare a tonic for you that I think you will like far better than the bitter medicine you gave Mr. Tufts.' He winked and smiled, then continued. 'When you have rested thoroughly, I hope you will agree to stay with us to supervise the baby's treatment. You will be our honored guest.'

Sarah smiled, but looked like she might cry at the same time. She wiped her eyes on her apron. "Did the baby survive?" she asked earnestly.

"Yes, he did," said Mollyockett proudly. "After that first sip of warm cow's milk he came to love it and cried for more. He grew to be a fine strong boy and I foresaw a great future for him. He is about six or seven years old now.

"The last time I visited his family I was pleased to see a sturdy, healthy boy about four years old. His head was covered with golden ringlets. I begged his mother to cut me a lock. She did and I still have it.

"After I put the lock of hair safely between two pieces of birch bark that I use to press herbs, I took the little boy on my lap. I told him he would be a great man. He looked at me solemnly, as if to agree. Then I offered advice that he was too young to understand. I hoped that his parents would remind him in later years of the words of the old Pequawket doctoress who saved his life."

Sarah's awe at Mollyockett's skill and wisdom expanded yet again. "What did you tell him, Mollyockett?"

Mollyockett smiled, recalling the rosy-cheeked little boy sitting on her lap and looking up at her. "I told him as I have told other good little boys,

Never marry a woman who does not love flowers.
Or trust a person who hates music or children.
When you find yourself in bad company, get out of it at once.
And remember that, as you pass through life's journey,
Your greatest troubles will be found to result from ignorance."

Sarah pondered this advice and then repeated it. "I want always to remember what you said. I think I will embroider a sampler and hang it over my bed so I will never forget." She thought a moment. "But what about me? What should the man I marry love?"

Mollyockett smiled affectionately at her caretaker. "Sarah, the man you marry should love animals and the forests, fields and lakes. He should give thanks for each day God gives him from dawn to starry night. Most of all he should love you, and that will be easy." She patted Sarah's hand still holding the sack of beads. Then she closed her eyes and fell asleep.

Chapter 13

As the days passed, Mollyockett grew weaker. She seldom had strength for anything more than a few words of conversation. Some times she spoke, but often in fragments that did not always make sense to Sarah. "Find the still waters. The sweet flag is there. Under the leaves the bloodroot hides. You must dig for its goodness. Metallak, Oozaluk, I have found a good place to rest. Hush, hush, tiny one. You are safe. Hail Mary, full of grace. Be with me now and at the hour of my death. Oh, I am so cold." These words confused and saddened Sarah. Other than her occasional utterances, Mollyockett slept most of the time. Sarah and the other women of Andover did their best to make her comfortable and keep her clean. Reverend Strickland visited and prayed over her still form. A profound sorrow filled Sarah's heart.

On Sunday morning, Sarah was pleased to see that Mollyockett seemed more alert and lucid. She decided to return later after church with a surprise. After breakfast, when Sarah had left for church, Mollyockett fell into a deep sleep. When she awoke she heard Sarah calling to her from the doorway. "Mollyockett, are you awake? I've brought someone to see you."

Mollyockett strained to raise her head and focused her eyes on the doorway. Silhouetted against the light she saw Sarah and behind her a taller figure with broad shoulders and dark hair. She narrowed her eyes to see better. "Piol, is that you?" she asked incredulously.

Sarah laughed nervously. Maybe this visit was a mistake. "No, Mollyockett," she answered. "I said I would bring my friend, James, to see you and here he is."

Mollyockett smiled at her own foolishness. Of course, it was not Piol. Piol was a mature man and this, she saw dimly, was a young man, still not grown into his height. "Forgive me, James. My mind wanders. Welcome. Well, now, what a happy surprise. Sarah says that you are a good farmer and expect someday to have your own homestead. Come in and sit. We'll talk for a while."

James cleared his throat nervously, "Pleased to meet you ma'am. If this isn't a good time, I can come back later."

Mollyockett shook her head. "No, no this is a fine time, a very fine time. Please sit down. There's a stool over there."

James shifted his weight and rolled his hat in his hands. "It's all right. I'll just stand. It seems like we've been sitting for hours in church."

Sarah straightened the blanket and asked, "Would you like me to make you some tea?"

"No, dear," Mollyockett replied, "but maybe James would like some."

James shook his head and said, "No, thank you. I can't stay long. I just wanted to meet the woman Sarah admires so much." He paused. "Who is this Piol you mentioned? Do I look like someone you know?"

Mollyockett smiled, "Piol is my son. You do resemble him as he was in his youth. How silly of me to confuse you with him. Now he is a grown man and a leader of my people. You may have heard of him. He is known as Captain Susup."

"Yes," replied James, "I believe I saw him in town in the spring. He's a big fellow with a scar on his chest."

"Yes, James. That is Piol, all right. He passes through from time to time. I expect he will come to visit me when he learns of my illness. He has always been a good son, though I worried about him when he was not much older than you. Most of the time he was a good boy. At other times he seemed often to be in the middle of bad situations. He called them adventures. I called them trouble."

Sarah said, "Mollyockett, you did tell me about when Piol was a baby and small child, but I guess I didn't think about what might have happened to him when he grew up."

Mollyockett smiled, "Well, he almost didn't grow up at all and surely would have died if I didn't know my medicines."

James stammered and then asked, "If it's not being too nosy, what kind of trouble did he get into?"

"Well," said Mollyockett, "you noticed that scar. I'll tell you how he got it. Unlike his father, who was my first husband, Piol had a strong liking for spirits, especially as a young man. He was drinking with a companion from Caratunk, a white man. They got into a drunken discussion of their ancestors. Piol, who usually did not boast, said that his mother was the daughter of chiefs and had a legitimate claim to all the land hereabouts. He also bragged of my medical skills.

"The white man, like Piol, had been drinking far too much and laughed at Piol's claims. Piol became angry and insulted the man by making foolish remarks about that young man's mother. They shoved each other. Then Piol pulled his knife. The young man grabbed his gun and shot a charge of buckshot into Piol's chest. Although badly wounded, Piol charged at him and the white man had to break the stock of his gun over Piol's head. Piol kept coming. Finally, the white man hit him so hard over the back that his gun barrel bent. At last, Piol fell and the white man, fearing trouble with the elders, left him for dead."

She paused while Sarah and James waited. James cleared his throat. This seemed to jog Mollyockett's attention. She resumed her story as if unaware of the interruption.

"Soon some of Piol's friends found him. When the young men saw the flesh of his chest gaping and pulsing with blood, they tried to revive him and stop the bleeding. They washed the wounds on his chest, head and back, but the bleeding continued. They tried to bind his scalp wound, but with no success. Luckily, one of them remembered that I was a healer and they brought him to me. At first, I was angry. 'What foolishness have you been into?' I asked. Then I noticed his pale skin and shallow breathing. I remembered his poor father. I set my mind. I would not lose this Piol.

"First, I packed the wounds with dry moss to staunch the bleeding. Then I gave him a burdock tea to strengthen his blood. When the bleeding had slowed, I carefully removed the moss and bathed the wounds with a witch hazel tonic. Using linen thread, I sewed the scalp wound loosely. He braved the pain by biting on a stick. I applied a poultice made of the inner bark of the hackmatak to prevent the festering that is common to such wounds. The next morning healing had begun, but the chest wound was swollen somewhat, so I made a salve of Solomon seal, extract of dandelion, mixed with rosin, beeswax and lard. I applied this several times a day until his wounds had healed and the sewing threads could be removed."

James was amazed, not only at Mollyockett's remarkable memory and medical skill, but also at the refusal of her son to give up when he was clearly beaten. "These are some tough people," he thought. Then he asked Mollyockett, "I guess he survived, but that was quite a beating. Some men would have been crippled or permanently injured after a thrashing like that."

Mollyockett nodded silently and closed her eyes. After a moment, she opened them again and was alert once more. "Thanks to God, he is now strong and healthy, but he will always carry with him the scar to serve as a reminder of foolish behavior. I hope it also reminds him of his mother's prayers and loving care. Since that time he has controlled his drinking and his temper and has become a leader among the Indian people. He's a good boy, a good boy."

She looked toward James. It was not clear whether she referred to Piol or Sarah's young man. She seemed confused herself. "This visit is welcome, but I'm afraid I need to sleep. Thank you both for coming. I will see you again." Her eyelids fluttered and her breathing became slow and deep. Sarah and James looked at each other. She took his hand and led him quietly out of the wigwam.

When she returned home, Sarah told her aunt that Mollyockett had confused James with her son, Piol, but then she seemed to recover herself. "She told us a good story, but she kept stopping and starting again. She seemed very worn out. I'm worried. I won't let her tire herself to amuse me again. I have grown so fond of Mollyockett and learned so much from her. She is so good. I pray God will protect her."

"Amen," said Aunt Sophia quietly. "Amen."

Mollyockett slept through the afternoon. Mrs. Merrill came by in the afternoon, and sat for a while, but Mollyockett did not awaken. She looked so peaceful when Sarah's aunt came by to bring her supper that Sophia decided not to rouse her.

In the middle of the night Mollyockett drifted out of her sleep into a strange state. She felt peculiar. The room, even in the darkened wigwam, seemed to wheel around her. She wondered, "What is happening to me?" She lost consciousness. Later she awoke again. She realized that her left side would not move. She found this experience curious, but not alarming.

Suddenly she was aware of being in the front of a canoe. She felt warm, as if wrapped in her white fur cape. As she rested easily against a wicker backrest, she sensed that a dark powerful figure sat behind her paddling with the current of a great rushing river. Huge pines lined the shore and the embankments were black with the thickness of them. The dark trees seemed to fly by. Moonlight illuminated the water rippling with white crested waves. The canoe moved rapidly down the silver stream. The pines gave way to giant cliffs that first loomed up on either side, then met overhead. The canoe seemed to be passing through a tunnel at great speed. The water roared as it passed through a stone chute.

Suddenly light appeared ahead. The canoe slowed and left the tunnel and moved into intense brightness. The canoe headed toward the land where a single white wigwam sat on the river bank. Loon cries filled the air. Mollyockett knew that the wigwam was her destination. She felt like an infant bundled in a down lined cradleboard, carried

Mollyockett's Gravestone

Fifty years after Mollyockett's death churchwomen of Andover erected a gravestone in Woodlawn Cemetery to mark the site of her burial. Her stone, decorated with greens and pinecones left by admirers, reads: "Mollockett, Baptised Mary Agatha, Died in the Christian Faith, August 2, 1816, The last of the Pequakets."

(Photo by the author)

along, protected and safe. She saw the tent flap open of its own accord. The white light encompassed her. Words filled her mind. "He leadeth me beside the still water, I will fear no evil, for thou art with me. Thy will be done, for thine is the power and the glory. Straight is the gate and narrow is the way that leadeth to life eternal, and few there be that find it. I can see the gate! I am on my way!"

Appendix A
Notes on How the Book was Written: Separating Fact from Fiction

1. The basic documented facts of Mollyockett's life are well summarized in Cathy Newell's excellent monograph, *Molly Ockett*.

2. Although I spent a lot of time in the Boston Public Library, the Massachusetts Historical Society and the Bethel Historical Society, made trips to Fryeburg, Paris and environs, Andover and Odanak, my research has been by no means exhaustive. One big disappointment is my failure to locate Colonel Clark, despite reviewing Massachusetts and Maine military records and Massachusetts census data for 1790 and 1810.

3. Various sources gave contradictory dates and places and relationships. I have tried to build a feasible chronology and surmise reasonable relationships. It is a work of fiction.

4. I confess that I sometimes implanted actual events or quotes from one situation into another speculative, imagined situation. Mea culpa!

5. I do know that some historians give her name as Molly Ockett and I know why that makes sense. There are many other spellings as well. Her gravestone reads "Mollockett." But when I say "Mollyockett," it seems to come out as one word. The same is true of Tomhegan.

6. Some of the Indian stories are my interpretation of stories I've read. The Glooscap story, "How the Weasel Got His White Winter Coat," I made up entirely.

7. I drew up a fairly detailed chronology using all the sources I had. Then I tried to reconcile conflicts and adopted one that I considered to be feasible. I know other sequences of events may be fully as arguable.

8. Little is known about Mollyockett's children, with the exception of Molly Susup, or about her first husband. In most cases, I have speculated on speculation. Likewise, little is known about her day to day relationship with Sabbatis or Metallak. I have built the story around what is known and imagined the rest.

9. Sarah is a fictional character, although the rest of the Bragg family were real people. Sacawewa's family and the events in Plymouth are entirely fictional.

Appendix B
Mollyockett Chronology

1738?	Mollyockett was born below the falls near Saco; her actual birth-date is unknown
1744	Mollyockett's family was said to be living in Scarborough
1744–1748	King George's war; Pequawkets split and divide support; Mollyockett's father (Werenmanhead, Saquant, Capt Sam?) decides to join with the English
1745	14 women and children, including Mollyockett, sent to Plymouth for safekeeping
1749	11 Abenakis returned to Falmouth, Maine to be at the peace treaty; Mollyockett and two other girls remain in Plymouth
1749–1750	Negotiations for the girls' return
1750	Mollyockett and the two other girls returned to Richmond on the Kennebec during the spring or summer
1755	French and Indian War begins
1755	Indians reported (by Mollyockett) to have buried gold in Paris before departing for Canada, marking the spot with two traps hung in a tree
1759	Rogers' Raid on St. Francis Mission; one of the boys taken was named Sabattis
1760s	Molly Peol reported to have had a child by Captain Swassin; this date can't be right since she was christened in 1764
1762–1763	First settlers move to Fryeburg; no Indians in the area at that time
1763	French lose Canada; treaty signed; Indians return to Androscoggin and Saco valleys
1764	May 31: Mollyockett's daughter, Marie Marguerite, was christened at St. Francis; father was Piol Susup (Pierre Joseph)
1766	One account reports marrriage of Mollyockett and Captain John Susup, another that she was living with Sabattis in Fryeburg. My guess is that Captain John was her son by Sabattis
1768	Susup, son of Mollyockett and Sabattis born; other children: Paseel (Basil), a daughter who married a white man and lived in Darby, Vermont; and a daughter who became the mother of Abbesqua
1769	Mollyockett returns to Fryeburg without Piol Susup

1769 ca	One source says Abbesqua was born; if she was Mollyockett's grandaughter, this cannot be true
1770's	700 Indians reported living in Maine and New Hampshire
1772	Henry Tufts records Mollyockett's kindness to a poor white man and his family
1772	Piol Susup, Mollyockett's first husband, recorded as having died sometime before this date
1772–1775	Henry Tufts visits Captain Swassin's group; seeks medical treatment from Mollyockett
1772 or later	Mollyockett stops living with Sabattis, joins Captain Swassin's group
1774 May	Mollyockett goes to Quebec to sell furs and buy husband's soul out of Purgatory
1776	After the American Revolution many Indians return to Canada; others were absorbed or served as guides, advisors to settlers
1780	Nathanial Segar visits Bethel, finds Indians friendly
1781 August	Tomhegan's raid on Bethel (Sudbury Canada); Sabattis guided relief party from Fryeburg; Mollyockett saves Colonel Clark
1788	Mollyockett living in Andover with family of Old Philip
1790 July	Mollyockett midwifes birth of first white child in Andover, a daughter of friend, Sarah Merrill
1798	Susup, Mollyockett's son badly injured; Mollyockett cures him
1799–1800	Mollyockett with group of Indians in Troy and Potten, Vermont, heals injured man; treats settlers ill due to outbreak of dysentery
1800	Mollyockett's daughter living with a white husband in Darby, Vermont
1806	Molly Peol and Peol's daughter, Ursula, baptized
1809	August 27: Hannibal Hamlin born; the following winter Mollyockett heals him on Paris Hill
1810	Captain Susup reported to be a chief in Canada
1816	Spring: Mollyockett becomes ill while camping with Metallak and others at Beaver Brook near Upper Richardson Lake (Lake Molechunkamunk). She was taken to Andover; Indians stayed for two weeks then left her in the care of the town; she died on August 2; 1816 was known as "the year with no summer"
1867	August 4: Woodlawn Cemetery, Andover; dedication of Mollyockett's gravestone; address by Nathaniel Tuckerman True

Appendix C

References

Barrows, John Stuart, *Fryeburg Maine, an Historical Sketch,* Pequawket Press, Fryeburg, Maine, 1938

Baxter, James Phinney, *The Pioneers of New France in New England,* Joel Munsel's Sons, Albany, New York, 1894 (Republished by Heritage Books, Bowie, Maryland, 1980)

Bean, Eva, "Abenakis," Handwritten notes (Bethel Historical Society Collection)

Bennett, Randall H., *Bethel Maine: An Illustrated History,* Bethel Historical Society, Inc., Bethel, Maine, 1991

Bennett, Randall H., *Oxford County, Maine: a Guide to Its Historic Architecture,* Oxford County Historic Resource Survey, Bethel, Maine, 1984

Bethel Historical Society, *The Bethel Courier,* Special Edition, August 3, 1981

Calloway, Colin G., "Algonkians in The American Revolution," in *Algonkians of New England: Past And Present,* Peter Barnes, Ed., Dublin Series For New England Folklife, Boston University, 1993

Calloway, Colin G., *The Abenaki,* Chelsea House Publishers, New York and Philadelphia, 1989

Calloway, Colin G., *After King Philip's War,* University Press of New England, Hanover and London, 1997

Coffin, The Reverend Paul, "Journals of His Missionary Tours," Maine Historical Society Collections IV, 1798

Cook David S., *Above the Gravel Bar: The Indian Canoe Routes of Maine,* Mill Printing Co., Milo, Maine, 1985

Demos, John, *The Unredeemed Captive,* Alfred A. Knopf, New York, 1994

Erdoes, Richard, and Alfonso Ortiz, Eds., *American Indian Myths and Legends,* Pantheon Books, New York, 1984

Ford, Raven Tom, Ed., *Indian Double Curve Secrets,* Audenreed Press, Brunswick, Maine, 1997

Hensler, Cristy Ann, *Guide to Indian Quillworking,* Hancock House, Blaine, Washington, 1989

Johnson, Charles Everett, *The Legends of Mollyockett,* Copyright 1995

Johnson, Steven F., *Ninnuok (the People),* Bliss Publishing Company, Marlborough, Massachusetts, 1995

Kimball, Richard, "Hannibal Hamlin Served In Time Of Crisis, Too," clipped article, no date (Bethel Historical Society Collection)

Leadbeater, Helen, "Molly Ocket: Sketch for 8/22/77 talk at Fryeburg Historical Society," typed notes (Bethel Historical Society Collection)

Leadbeater, Helen, "Notes on Birch Box made by Molly Ocket," accompanied by photo of similar basket lost from Maine Historical Society and purse, also made by Mollyockett (Bethel Historical Society Collection)

Leadbeater, Helen, "References for Molly Ocket Paper by Helen M. Leadbeater 1977," typed notes (Bethel Historical Society Collection)

Leadbeater, Helen, Letter to Stanley Howe, comments on Molly Ockett draft, May 1, 1981 (Bethel Historical Society Collection)

Leadbeater, Helen, Typed notes on Lovewell's Raid, May 19, 1725, May 17, 1975 (Bethel Historical Society Collection)

Leadbeater. Helen, Letter to Eva Bean, commenting on her text, "Molly Ockett," September 6, 1966 (Bethel Historical Society Collection)

Leavitt, Robert M., and David A. Francis, Eds., *Kolusuwakonol: Philip S. LeSourd's English and Passamaquoddy-Maliseet Dictionary,* Passamaquoddy-Maliseet Bilingual Program, Pleasant Point, Perry, Maine, 1986, produced by Audio-Forum, Jeffrey Norton, Guilford, Connecticut

Leland, Charles G., *Algonquin Legends,* Dover Publications, New York, 1992

Maine Historical Society Collections, First Series, Vol. 4, pp. 145-167

Mason, Ellen McRoberts, "The Town of Conway," Granite Monthly, Vol. 20, No. 6, June, 1896, pp. 358-9

McBride, Bunny, and Harold Prins, "Molly Ockett, Pigwacket Doctor," in *Northeastern Indian Lives,* Robert S. Gruymet, Ed., University of Massachusetts Press, Amherst, Massachusetts, 1996

McBride, Bunny, *Women of the Dawn,* University of Nebraska Press, Lincoln and London,1999

McMullen, Ann, "Native Basket Styles and Changing Group Identity In Southern New England," in *Algonkians of New England: Past And Present,* Peter Barnes, Ed., Dublin Series For New England Folklife, Boston University, 1993, pp.76-88

Moorhead, Robert M, "Moll Locket," *The Western Mainer,* Vol. 1, No. 4, December 17, 1970

Newell, Catherine S-C., *Molly Ockett,* Bethel Historical Society, Bethel, Maine, 1981

Nicholas, Joseph A., and David A. Francis, Eds., *Passamaquoddy Brief Histories,* Copyright by Passamaquoddy Tribal Council, Perry, Maine, 1988, published by Audio-Forum, Jeffrey Norton, Guilford, Connecticut

Noyes, Bernice, and Agnes Haines, "Last Indian Raid Upon Bethel Settlement, August 3, 1781," as reported to the Bethel Historical Society (typescript in Bethel Historical Society Collection)

Parkman, Francis, *France and England in North America ,*Vol. II, Library of America, 1983

Poor, Agnes Blake, as told and revised by Sylvanus Poor, *Andover Memorials,* 1883, Copy of typescript (Bethel Historical Society Collection)

Registre Des Baptemes, Mariages, Sepultures, St. Francois-du-Lac, 31 Mai 1764, Museum of Religion in Nicolet, Quebec (record of Marie Marguerite's baptism)

Rich, Louise Dickinson, "Molly Ockett," *Woman's Day,* no date visible, clipped copy and hand copied article (Bethel Historical Society Collection)

Russell, Howard S., *Indian New England Before the Mayflower,* University Press of New England, Hanover and London, 1980

Starbird, Charles M., *The Indians of the Androscoggin Valley, Lewiston Journal* Printshop, 1928

Stark, James Henry, *Antique Views of Boston,* Theodore Thomte, Ed., Burdette and Company, Boston, 1967

Sumner, Samuel, "History of Missisco Valley 1860," quoted in Nathaniel Tuckerman True's Maine Historical Society article, printed in the *Oxford Democrat,* January 2, 1863.

Tapley, Mark, "Mol Lockett, the Last Squaw of the Androscoggin Tribe," Daily Lewiston Journal, April 6, 1889

The Friday Club, *Andover, the First 175 Years,* Andover, Maine, 1979, Chapter 1, Indians, Chapter 2, Early White Settlers, Chapter 5, Churches

True, Nathaniel Tuckerman, *History of Bethel,* Heritage Books, Bowie, Maryland, 1994

True, Nathaniel Tuckerman, "The Last of the Pequakets: Mollocket," written for the Maine Historical Society, *Oxford Democrat,* January 2 1863, reprinted in The Bethel Courier, Vol. II, No. 2, June 1978

Tufts, Henry, *Narratives of the Life, Adventures, Travels and Sufferings of Henry Tufts, now residing at Lemington, in the District of Maine. In substance, as Compiled From his Own Mouth,* 1807, reprinted in 1930 as *The Autobiography of a Criminal*

Ulrich, Laurel Thatcher, *A Midwife's Tale: The Life of Martha Ballard, Based on Her Diary, 1785–1812,* Vintage Books, Random House, New York, 1991

Ulrich, Laurel Thatcher, *The Age of Homespun,* Alfred A. Knopf, New York, 2001

Wilbur, C. Keith, *The New England Indians,* The Globe Pequot Press, Chester, Connecticut, 1978

Wilkins, Martha Fifield, Randall Bennett, Ed., *Sunday River Sketches,* 1977

Wright, Meredith, *Everyday Dress of Rural America, 1783–1800,* Dover Publications, New York, 1992

_____, "Legend Of Norway's Beautiful Lake," *Lewiston Journal,* November 12-16, 1904

_____, "Sources" (on Mollyockett) (Bethel Historical Society Collection)

_____, "The Curse of Mollockett," poem and commentary (Bethel Historical Society Collection)

_____, "Last Home of Mollyockett," *Lewiston Journal,* undated found in Charles Scrapbook #1, Fryeburg Library, 1910-13, Interview with Anna Marston

_____, "Moll Ockett, The Abandoned, and the First White Settlers of Andover," *Lewiston Journal Magazine Section,* July 28, 1917 (Bethel Historical Society Collection)

 Pat Stewart is a graduate of Douglass College, Rutgers University and holds a Masters and a Doctorate from Harvard University. She has written a book on decorative painting, *Brush, Sponge, Stamp*, with Paula DeSimone and maintains a studio in her home on Indian Pond, Greenwood, Maine, where she paints and writes. She is married to Henry Stewart, a mediator and arbitrator, and has three children: Darnley, a lawyer; Tyler, owner of an independent book store; and Tory, a playwright.